RON LOVELL

Dangerous Decisiones

A LORENZO MADRID MYSTERY

FIRST Edition
Penman Productions, Gleneden Beach, Oregon
Copyright © 2018, 2022 by Ronald P. Lovell

The events, people, and incidents in this story are the sole product
of the author's imagination. The story is fictional and any resemblance to
individuals living or dead is purely coincidental.

Printed in the United States of America
Library of Congress Control Number: 2018935840
ISBN: 978–1–953517–11–1

Cover design: Suzanne Parrott
Book designer: Liz Kingslien
Cover photo credits: *Statue of Lady Justice,* iStockphoto.com
Chapter opener/end art credits: Shutterstock.com

P.O. Box 400, Gleneden Beach, Oregon 97388
RonLovellAuthor.com

DEDICATION

To my mother, Verna Lovell, and my grandmother,
Lora Bickerton who made me what I am today.

THANK YOU

*Although the idea for Lorenzo Madrid is my
own, neither he nor I could exist without the help
of close friends, all of whom I want to thank.*

- *Linda Hosek, for the idea of Maxine March. I filled in
  the fictional details of her life, but Linda helped flesh
  her out as a character and also saved her from death—at
  my novelist's hand—many times.*
- *Nick Sharma, for suggesting the plot of "Innocent," out
  of which grew the character of Lorenzo Madrid, and for
  being a great business partner.*
- *Juan, Eulalia, Daniel, Rafa, and Madeline Perez, for
  help with Spanish words and phrases and helping me
  become an "honorary Mexican."*
- *Liz Kingslien, my designer, who turns my words on paper
  into books that look wonderful from cover to cover, and
  for long years of our working together on many projects.*
- *Mardelle Kunz, my editor, who unfortunately could not
  work on this particular book, has made sure on previous books that the words made sense and were spelled
  and used correctly. I owe her a lot for rescuing me from
  many plot and grammatical miscues.*

— Ron Lovell

"If a little knowledge is dangerous,
where is the man who has so much
as to be out of danger."

— Thomas Huxley

1

MOST NIGHTS, LORENZO MADRID HAD TROUBLE GOING TO SLEEP, let alone resting for the six or seven hours experts said were vital to good health. Too many concerns were always racing through his head—his law practice, his godson Tito, his own health. Often, in the wee hours of the morning, the old symptoms of PTSD returned with a vengeance: night sweats, nightmares, a racing heart.

Tonight had been different. He was sleeping soundly when the buzz on his cell phone woke him. Calls at 4 a.m. did not usually bring good news.

He turned on a lamp and answered the phone. "Hello."

"Lorenzo Madrid?"

He sat up in bed and swung his legs around so his feet were touching the floor. "Yes, this is Lorenzo Madrid. Who's calling, please?"

"You don't know me, and I apologize for waking you. You sound pretty sleepy."

Lorenzo didn't want to seem rude, but this guy needed to get to the point. "Who's calling, please?" he repeated.

"Oh, sorry. This is Kurt Jenkins. I'm the second secretary at the American embassy in Quito, Ecuador."

"Ecuador?"

The word cleared all the remaining cobwebs from Lorenzo's brain. "You're calling about my friend, Maxine March."

"As a matter of fact I am. I'll be blunt. She's in a women's prison down here and is not doing very well. Let's just say a friend of hers gave me your name as a close friend in the U.S. I might call."

"Yes, we are friends." Hardly close friends but she had dropped, quite literally, into his lap several months before and then disappeared, leaving a little boy for him to care for. If Maxine had given this government official his name, she obviously needed help.

"Prison? What did she do to be sent to prison?"

"I'll fax you the official report. Are you a Spanish speaker?"

With a name like Lorenzo Madrid, what else could I be, Lorenzo thought, but did not say. "Yes, I speak and read Spanish, but I'm maybe a little rusty at it."

"Of course. Your name alone should . . . because, of course, the documents I will send you are in Spanish."

"You were saying, Mr. Jenkins."

"Oh, yes, of course. Basically, she is charged with kidnapping an Ecuadorian boy . . ." Jenkins paused and Lorenzo heard a rustling of papers. "Here it is. A boy named Tito. I don't have a last name."

"She mentioned him when I last saw her." Mentioned him, hell, she had left him behind for him to take care of.

At that moment, Tito appeared in the doorway, rubbing his eyes. "Papa."

Lorenzo put a finger to his lips and motioned for the boy to sit beside him. Tito ran over and snuggled close to him.

"Yes, yes, go on, please."

"Ms. March denies the kidnapping now and said, at first, that she was looking into the procedure for adopting an Ecuadorian child for close friends in the U.S. But the immigration police already had her in their sights for what they call a kidnapping. In coming here, she walked into a trap they had happily laid. Kidnapping anywhere is a serious crime, of course, but because it is an American woman taking a child from his country, no matter her motive, the local authorities want to make an example of her.

There will be a trial, and I'm sure it will be a spectacle. Do you remember the case of Lori Berenson who was accused of aiding the Shining Path guerillas in Peru 20 years or so ago?"

"Yes. She was tried and convicted and sentenced to years in a particularly bad prison high in the Andes where she nearly died of a whole number of ailments she caught up there."

"That's the case," said Jenkins. "And it became a show trial exemplifying Yankee imperialism at its worse. We don't want that to happen to Maxine March. That's why I called you. I've visited Ms. March two times. At first, she would barely speak to me, but on the second visit, she relaxed and told me about you and the boy and how she had left him in your care when she came down here."

Lorenzo hesitated before answering. After all, immigration agents were rounding up brown-skinned people all over the U.S. on a daily basis, and many of them who had led exemplary lives in the U.S. for many years, were being deported for no crime other than the color of their skin. Lorenzo pulled Tito closer to him.

"Mr. Jenkins, I don't know you but I guess I have to trust you because it sounds like I'm going to need to help Maxine. And you'll be the key to getting me into seeing her. Everything you said is true. I have the boy."

"Mr. Madrid, you have no reason to trust me. Right now, I'm just a voice on the phone who woke you out of a sound sleep. But I want to assure you that our conversation is confidential. One of my duties in the diplomatic service—like all of my coworkers—is to look after the well-being of Americans in the countries we are assigned to. Maxine March is in bad trouble here and, from what she told me, you may be the only person who can help her. I am on her side, and if you agree to what I would like you to do, I'll be on your side too."

Lorenzo squeezed Tito, who buried his face in his arm.

"Okay, great. You're an attorney, right?" asked Kurt.

"Yes, I am."

"General practice?"

"I've just set up a general practice in a college town in Oregon."

"Eugene, the U of O?"

"No, Corvallis, Oregon State. I went to law school at UCLA and I taught there too. One of my specialties is immigration law."

"Hallelujah!" shouted Jenkins. "This is turning out better than I thought it would."

"What do you propose I do?"

"You'll need to come down here to size things up. If it's possible, you need to represent her in court."

"I can't practice in another country. I'd have no standing."

"Let me look into that. I think it would be possible if you had a local attorney to act as co-counsel. Although certain elements of this government acted improperly in this instance, it is a nation with a code of laws and standards of justice. It is not some tin-pot, lawless dictatorship." Lorenzo was quiet for a few moments. "Mr. Madrid. Are you still there?"

"I need a moment."

From the start Lorenzo had known that the day would come when he would have to face the reality that Tito was not his son. He would always want to be a part of Tito's life. But that little life was in jeopardy now and always would be as long as his legal status was uncertain. He was, after all, a kind of fugitive from his own country. Maxine had tried to do her best for him, however badly it had turned out. She needed Lorenzo now and so did Tito.

"Okay, I'll do it for Maxine and the boy," said Lorenzo. "But I need time to sort this out. I have pending cases, I'll need to arrange for care of the boy, and I'll need to figure out my legal strategy. Also, how I'll pay for this."

"A few days?"

"A week at the minimum."

"Agreed. I've got some unofficial connections that will help us. A bright, young guy—Alberto Dragón—who we use for lots of things here at the embassy. He speaks perfect English. I guess you could call him a fixer, for want of a better word."

"What about the co-counsel?"

"I'll talk to our legal attaché about that."

"Any thoughts about the money to pay for all of this?"

"I've got an idea about that too," said Jenkins. "I'm going to send you a text with a phone number you'll need to memorize and then erase. Call it and you'll be told what to do next. I'll be in touch."

Both men ended the call and Lorenzo sat on the edge of the bed hugging the little boy ever tighter.

"Are you crying, Papa?" Tito asked.

Lorenzo wiped his eyes. "Only from being weak from hunger."

"What is hunger, Papa?"

"When you haven't had any food and your stomach starts growling like a lion until you fill it up." Then he picked the boy up and carried him out of the room, amid shrieks of laughter from both of them.

Lorenzo sat the boy down on the kitchen counter and pulled out a mixing bowl, flour, eggs, and milk. "Does anyone around here want pancakes?" he said, looking quizzically at Tito.

"I do!" shouted the boy.

"Well, I guess that settles it. Pancakes it will be for my little *amigo.*"

"Can your tired old papa have at least one pancake?"

"*Un poco,*" said the boy, holding a thumb and forefinger up. "*Un poco poco.*"

"We'll just have to see about that," he said, as he started mixing the flour with the other ingredients.

As he said that, Tito reached across the counter and hugged Lorenzo tightly. "I love you, Papa."

In the distance, Lorenzo heard the buzz from his cell phone to signify that a new message was coming through.

2

AFTER BREAKFAST, Lorenzo and Tito dressed and drove downtown to his office. Tito's school was in a room next door. There he had a normal looking classroom with a desk and play area and shelves full of books surrounding the room on three sides. Lorenzo had also hired a full-time teacher, an Irish woman named Josephine O'Brien, who Tito called "Miss Jo." The boy adored her and she was good, with experience as a nanny for a number of British and American families in England. She had moved to the U.S. to take care of a sister who had recently died. Given Tito's uncertain legal status, Lorenzo couldn't enroll him in school yet.

She fitted in well with Lorenzo's group of friends who allowed him to deal with his complicated life. Chief among these was Sam Lincoln, a young Black man who Lorenzo hired in L.A. and brought to Oregon to help him in the office as his paralegal. Sam attended law school part-time. He was smart and adaptable to Lorenzo's ever-changing life. He loved Tito and the boy felt the same about him.

Tito rushed up the stairs and ran down the hall to the classroom. Jo was waiting for him at the doorway. "And how is Master Tito this morning?" she said in her slight Irish brogue.

"I think I want to be called *Señor Tito*," the boy said, his eyes sparkling mischievously. "That is my real language."

"Oh, you do, do you? So we're going to be a little cheeky this morning, are we?" she said. "We'll see about that!" Then she picked him up and carried him into the classroom amid a torrent of giggles from him and laughter from her.

As she closed the door, Lorenzo leaned in to talk to her. "I need to talk to you about something a bit later this morning," he whispered.

Lorenzo walked down the hall to the small two-rooms that were his law office suite. Sam was reading what was certainly a law book.

"Morning, boss. How's everything today?"

"More complicated than usual, I'm afraid."

"Not sure I like the sound of that!"

"I'll fill you in after I make a phone call."

Lorenzo walked into his office and closed the door. He had decided to tell Sam and Jo all about the phone call from Ecuador. Without the two of them, he couldn't do what he had just agreed to do.

He sat down at his desk and looked at the contact information Jenkins had texted him. He had written down the terse language he had been told to use. He called on his land line phone, thinking it was less likely to be monitored than his cell. The area code was unfamiliar to him.

It rang for a long time before a gruff-voiced woman answered. "Comanche Enterprises."

"Yes, I was given this number to inquire about travel arrangements for a trip I will be making to Ecuador."

"Access number, please."

"LM 17."

"One moment please and I will connect you."

"Operations." A man's voice was younger but no more friendly than the woman's.

"My name is . . ."

"No names. What is your access number?"

Lorenzo gave it to him and waited until the voice said, "Here it is. Are you in a secure location?"

"My office in a room by myself."

"Hang up, and I will call you back."

Lorenzo did so, stood up, and walked to the door to the reception room holding his phone. When it rang, Lorenzo picked it up immediately, signaling to Sam not to do so. He walked into his office and sat down at his desk.

"Okay, that seems about as secure as we can make it under these circumstances." Lorenzo heard a rustling of papers before the man spoke again.

"I have your file," said the man. "My notes say that you will be traveling to Quito, Ecuador and need the proper visa to enter. You have a valid passport, I presume?"

"Yes," said Lorenzo, as he pulled his passport out of a locked desk drawer and opened it.

"You will need some documentation that authorizes you to practice law in Ecuador?"

"Yes, I will. I guess this assignment will involve that, but it is primarily a rescue mission for a . . . ."

"No details. I need to stick to logistics. What you do there is for others to decide."

"You will also be given a credit card and $10,000 in cash before you leave your current location. Once you are in Ecuador, you will be contacted by our people there."

"Can you tell me who is responsible for all of this, I mean the funding, the authorizations, the people I'll meet down there?

"That's beyond my pay grade. You will figure it out in time. One thing I will say, you can trust the people behind this. Just go there and the rest will unfold."

Lorenzo hung up the phone, then immediately dialed Jenkins' number at the embassy. A recorded message came on immediately.

"This is Kurt Jenkins, second secretary of the American embassy in Quito, Ecuador. I will be away from my office for the next few days. If this is urgent, please call the main number of the embassy."

MAXINE MARCH COULD BARELY KEEP TRACK of what day of the week it was. Most days, she tried to spend as much time as possible in the large room where inmates were allowed to gather when they weren't on work details. Since her arrival at the prison, she had worked in the laundry beside her two cell mates: Dawn Young, the unofficial head of the so-called "international" section of the prison, and the huge, tattoo-covered Sandra (last name unknown) who brought her clothes and towels and blankets. Most evenings, she had also been teaching English to inmates and some guards.

Because all of the women here had been arrested for real or contrived drug charges, they were not considered violent. As a result, prison officials, and even most of the guards, left them alone.

"Don't rock any boats," both Dawn and Sandra had said to Maxine on her first day here. And she had followed that advice, although she occasionally asked to speak to an official of the American embassy in Quito.

One morning, Gustavo Montez, a guard they all liked because he was helpful and very handsome, approached Maxine in the laundry as she was bent over a board ironing an officer's uniform. He had not been on duty for several weeks and everyone wondered what had happened to him.

"I need to talk to *Señorita* March,"

he said to the mean-faced woman trustee in charge of the laundry. He flashed a paper in her direction but did not wait for her to read it. "Official business." The woman nodded and pointed to a small storage room next to the larger laundry area. "In there, but keep the door open, *por favor.*"

Maxine followed Gustavo into the room. "It is good to see you, Gustavo. We were all worried about you. You've been gone for more than a week."

"Ten days exactly," he said. "There was some unpleasantness at one of the side gates. I was not involved directly, but I saw it all."

"Saw what?" asked Maxine.

Gustavo lowered his voice and glanced at the door.

"I should not tell you any of this but you are my friend and I want to help you. Of all the others in here, most are tough, hard women. But you are different. I appreciate it that you are teaching me and others English. That will help me get promoted."

"Your English was already very good," she said, wanting him to say more, but deciding it was best to wait him out.

"Okay. I have two things to say. Number one, an official of the American embassy is coming to see you tomorrow." He glanced at a slip of paper in his hand. "A *Señor* Kurt Jenkins."

"He's a high official in the embassy," she said, her relief causing her to cry. "Thank God, someone is watching out for me at last. He came to see me a few weeks ago but nothing happened."

"I don't know anything about his visit," said Gustavo. "They just asked me to tell you so you could prepare."

That's a switch, thought Maxine. No one seemed to care anything about her during the weeks she had been there.

"I'll be as ready as I can be in a place like this," she said disdainfully. Suddenly, she was seized by violent coughing. For a moment, she could not get her breath.

Gustavo jumped up and handed her a bottle of water.

"Drink this, *señorita.*" He handed her the water and watched her gulp it down. "Slowly, slowly."

The water helped stop the coughing.

"You need *medicina,*" he said. "You need to see the doctor."

"I couldn't trust any doctor in here. He'd be what we call a 'quack.'"

Gustavo looked perplexed. "What is 'quack?'"

She smiled. "That means someone who doesn't know anything more about being a doctor than a duck."

"Maybe so but you need help. I can see that with my plain eyes."

"I'll be fine," she said. "Can you get me some cough medicine? And cough drops?"

"I will try to do so."

"*Gracias.* You said you had two things to talk to me about."

"Yes, yes. Sorry."

Gustavo stood up and closed the door to the small room. "Ten days ago, there was an attempt to set you free from this place."

"Rescue me? From here?" Maxine started crying again, not the occasional tears but loud sobbing. "Oh, my God," she shouted. "Someone cares about me and knows I am here. I can't believe it. After all this time, there is hope."

Gustavo reached across the table and patted her hand. At that moment, another, more senior, guard, a fat and slovenly guy who was always harsh in how he treated the women, burst into the room.

"LIEUTENANT MONTEZ! YOU ARE FORGETTING YOUR DUTIES! GO TO MY OFFICE!"

Gustavo got up and left the room without uttering another word, leaving Maxine distraught. "He was telling me about my visitor. Tomorrow? Do you know of this?"

"Everyone in the prison knows of this," he said. "If you don't quit causing trouble, there will be no visit for you tomorrow or anytime!"

Amidst the onset of more coughing, Maxine left the room. She seemed on the verge of collapse as she entered the laundry until both Dawn and Sandra rushed over to steady her.

"Come on, baby girl," said Sandra, soothingly. "We need to get you in your bed."

"GET ME SOME MEDS!" she shouted over her shoulder.

ONCE HE SAW THAT LORENZO WAS OFF THE PHONE, Sam knocked gently, then opened the door. "You okay, boss?"

"Yeah, I think. Get us some coffee and come in."

Sam returned in seconds holding two cups, steam wafting from them. He looked at Lorenzo with an expectant look on his face. "This has to be bad news," he said. "You're letting me go. You're tired of this smart-ass Black guy opening his mouth when he should keep it shut."

Lorenzo sipped the brew. "God, no. Because of what I'm going to tell you, I'll need you and Jo more than ever."

"Whew, that's a relief!" Sam said, shaking his head.

"Okay, here's the story. I got a call early this morning from an official at the American embassy in Quito, Ecuador."

"No shit? I mean, no fooling?"

"He told me that Maxine Marsh has been in a prison down there for several weeks."

"My God! What's the charge?"

"Kidnapping of Tito."

"God no. I guess you could call it that, but she was saving his life. Besides that spooky guy . . . "

"Paul Bickford."

"Yeah, him. He did it and brought the boy here. She was already back in the U.S."

"Those details were conveniently

misplaced. Besides, she was there and he wasn't. She walked right into a trap. The authorities were waiting for her. I don't know the details but she is locked up in a women's prison that has to be like hell on earth."

"So, let me guess. You're going down there to save her. And you want me and Jo to take care of the boy."

"You got it, kid. Maybe only for a week. She'll go to trial and I've got to become her lawyer and try to get the charges dropped—for her and the boy."

"I shouldn't say this because you're my boss, but . . ."

"I know what you're going to say. I should have tried to find out what she was doing down there. I thought the whole thing was dangerous and foolish. After all, she left Tito without hesitating or even telling him she was leaving. Not all that motherly."

"And I took him without telling you," said Sam. "So I was part of this too. And you were pretty pissed off at me."

"Only for a day or so. I know you did what any compassionate person would do. Of course, we've all grown to love the boy. I'm at the point where I don't know what I'd do without him."

"Speaking frankly, boss, you may be about to find out."

"I've got to admit that I haven't tried to contact her or that I even cared what she was doing in Ecuador. But Tito never asks about her. Like other little kids who have had it rough, he has had to adjust to whatever happens."

"So now you're going to a strange place and into a foreign court where you don't know the system and try to save a woman you are less than friendly with," said Sam. "Shee-it, and then some!"

"I know I can count on you to help me, Sam."

"No question, boss. After what you've done for me, anything."

"I plan to tell all of this to Jo once we're finished talking. Would you want to move into my house, so the boy's life is not disrupted?"

"I can do that, sure."

"Jo can continue his studies and maybe cook for the two of you. I plan to go to Ecuador for a week or less to figure things out and then head back here to plot my strategy."

"What about your clients? A paralegal/law student like me ain't gonna' cut it with them."

"I'll get continuances for the court dates and call the others, pleading the need to handle a personal matter."

"How about your old pal Thaddeus? He'd do anything for you, boss." Sam hesitated and smiled.

"Go on, Sam, say what you're thinking."

"I was going to say he'd do anything to get you back in bed with him, at least once in a while."

Lorenzo smiled. "What? Did the two of you have a talk, 'brotha' to 'brotha'?"

"Something like that," said Sam. "One time, when we were waiting for you, and after a couple of drinks, he told me he was in love with you."

"He's told me that too. We had a one-night stand a couple of years ago but that was it. He's very smart and very good looking, but I just can't get involved with anyone right now. There's too much going on in my life."

"How long has it been since your old lover was killed?"

"Scott? Over ten years, I guess. Maybe more."

"I may be overstepping some boundaries here, boss, but isn't it time to think of yourself?"

"Maybe so, Sam, maybe so."

"You want me to get Jo in here? I can watch the boy."

"Yes, please. And thanks, Sam, for understanding all of this. I couldn't do what I'm about to do without you."

✪ ✪ ✪ ✪ ✪

Jo O'Brien took his news in stride. "You've got to help that poor woman, sir. She was very foolish to go off like she did and leave

16

the boy, even though she felt it was in his best interest. No woman should go into a country like that alone. Too dangerous! She's lucky you were here to take Tito."

"And I'm lucky that you came along to become his teacher. And Sam to be his protector and good friend."

"You know, sir, it is all well and good for me to teach him here, but someday soon, he'll need to go to a real school. With other kiddies his own age."

"I've been worrying about that too, Jo," said Lorenzo, a troubled look on his face. "That's why I've got to get Maxine out of prison and back here. Tito's status is so uncertain that I can't enroll him in school. He has no passport or papers of any kind."

"You can count on me, sir."

▢ ▢ ▢ ▢ ▢

Thaddeus Sampson, Lorenzo's old friend and, for a brief time, lover, readily accepted his invitation to dinner that night. Lorenzo set the time for eight so he could feed Tito, supervise his bath, and get him to bed at his usual time. They answered the door together.

Thad's face lit up when he saw the two of them standing there. "Aren't you a good looking pair of Latin heartbreakers."

He hugged Lorenzo and bent down to shake Tito's hand.

"*Buenos días, Señor* Thad. What is 'heartbreaker'?" The boy bowed and giggled before rushing away.

Lorenzo and Thad embraced again, with Thad squeezing a bit too tightly. "I've missed you," he whispered.

"Me too. Come in. I'll pour you some wine."

Thad walked into the living room and sat down as Lorenzo handed him a glass. Lorenzo held out his arms and Tito rushed in and jumped into them. "Tito wanted to say good night. He's got a big day tomorrow. His teacher . . ."

"Miss Jo," added Tito.

"Yes, Miss Jo. She and my assistant Sam are taking him to the zoo in Portland."

"Great, Tito. You'll have a good time seeing all the animals. What's your favorite?"

Tito stroked his chin before answering. "That tall one with a very long neck."

"A giraffe. Why him?"

"Because up high like that he can see danger ahead."

¤ ¤ ¤ ¤ ¤

Lorenzo avoided the main reason for his invitation to Thad until they had finished the take-out Thai dinner. Lorenzo stood up. "More wine?"

Thad remained quiet while Lorenzo outlined his plans.

"You're into this way too deep, Renzo," he said when he was finished. "You're risking a lot, both here—with the boy and your new law practice—but also the danger of going to a foreign country where you don't know the laws or how even to function every day. Your good looks and ability to speak Spanish will only get you so far."

"I know that, but I have to do it. For the boy's future . . ."

"And your own."

"Yes, for my own."

"Do you love this woman who you barely know? I mean will you wind up marrying her for the sake of the boy!"

"God no. Never."

"That's a relief," laughed Thad.

"I'll get her out of prison if I can and then see what happens. She's in no position to care for him now or maybe ever. I'll sort that out later. Maybe the boy can decide. I'm not sure. I've only known about all of this since this morning."

"I'll help you by helping Sam deal with your cases. You'll be gone for a week, right?"

"Yeah. Just to see how things are. I'll then need to return to Ecuador later."

"There are conditions for me to do this for you," he said with a grin as he stood up.

"I know, I know, Thad. Not tonight. The boy is in the other room! I can't do it. I appreciate your help as always, but not tonight."

5

DAWN AND SANDRA PUT MAXINE IN BED as soon as they helped her to their cell. They rubbed her body with some kind of bad-smelling herb mixture and forced some pills down her throat. After she slept for a few hours, they woke her up and gave her hot broth with pieces of what tasted like chicken but was probably the meat of some animal they had smuggled in from the jungle surrounding the prison. It tasted good and Maxine was in no position to argue. She sat on the side of her cot.

"I feel a lot better," she said. "Whatever you did for me, it worked. What was I eating? And did you rub something on my body?"

"You don't want to know the details, honey lamb," laughed Sandra. "We try a lot of stuff to survive in here. Sometimes it works and sometimes it doesn't."

"You've only got a few hours to get ready for your meeting with the counsel," said Dawn. "I scrounged around and found you a dress to wear."

She handed Maxine a cotton dress. "Try this on to see if it fits."

Maxine took off her smelly prison smock and slipped the dress over her head. "What do you think?" She turned around as if she was a model about to walk down a fashion show runway.

"Lookin' good," said Sandra.

"See how this works," said Dawn, as

she handed Maxine a wool shawl.

She draped it over her shoulders and her body shuddered at the sudden warmth. "My God, I feel almost human again," said Maxine. "I need a mirror to see if I can do something with my face. No makeup, not even a comb."

"*Voila!*" said Dawn, as she pulled both from a canvas bag. She also handed Maxine a tube of lipstick.

While Dawn worked on her face, Sandra started combing her hair. "Lots of rat's nests and tangles. Wu-eee! What a mess!"

After she finished this initial combing, Sandra produced a pair of scissors and began to cut Maxine's hair. Although she had worn her hair long for many years, Maxine didn't resist as the strands of hair rolled down her shoulders and onto the cement floor.

After a few more minutes, Sandra stepped back to appraise her handiwork. She handed Maxine the tiny mirror. "What do you think, baby girl?"

Although the mirror was cracked and murky, she could make out her head and shoulders. She turned to both of them with tears in her eyes. "You two are the best friends I've ever had. Thank you so much. I'll never be able to repay you."

"Just get out of this hell hole and tell the world about us," said Dawn. "No one knows we're even here!"

◻ ◻ ◻ ◻ ◻

A half hour later, Gustavo appeared at the doorway to the cell. "It's time to go, *señorita*. You look very nice. The representative of your government will be impressed."

Sandra walked up to Gustavo and rubbed against him. "You ever gonna' say that about me?"

Gustavo smiled and pulled away, looking embarrassed.

"Leave the poor man alone," said Dawn, shaking her head in dismay.

"Where's the creepy guy who hassled you earlier?" said Sandra.

"The major has a day off," he said. "I'm in charge of this part of the prison for the next few days."

He turned to Maxine. "We need to go, *Señorita* Marsh." And they did, crossing a courtyard and into another building.

Gustavo led Maxine down a long hall and into a room with large windows and a view of a river. A long conference table sat in the middle of the room with chairs lined up on both sides, as precise as soldiers in formation. Halfway down on either side, two chairs had been pulled out. Gustavo pointed to the closest one. Maxine walked over to it and sat down.

Minutes later, a door on the opposite side of the room opened and Kurt Jenkins walked in carrying a briefcase. The guard who had escorted him left the room at Gustavo's signal. "I will leave the two of you to discuss your business," he said to Jenkins. "I will be outside the door if you need me to assist in any way." He nodded to both of them and left the room.

"Are all the guards that polite?" said Jenkins, while pointing to the ceiling as if to warn her that the room was bugged.

"Yes, I've been treated very well," she said, shaking her head vigorously and making a thumbs-down gesture with both hands.

"That's good to hear," he said. "I will report that to my superiors." He motioned for her to walk toward the back wall of the room, which had no windows or light fixtures or anything else that might contain a bug. "I have brought the finale to that classical music recording you asked me to bring you."

Jenkins pulled a small CD player out of his briefcase and sat it on the table. He pushed a CD into the slot and soon, Tchaikovsky's *1812 Overture* finale filled the room. "We needed a diversion for our listeners," he whispered. "I am sure the walls of this room, to coin a phrase, have ears."

She nodded in agreement.

"I have contacted someone in Oregon whom you know and who has agreed to help us, Lorenzo Madrid."

"Thank God!" she said, a look of relief on her face. "He's

watching Tito, my son. But how did you know to get in touch with him?"

"I can't say anything more now for security reasons," said Jenkins. "Let's say that I was made aware of your involvement with him and called him."

"Made aware how? Did Paul . . ."

He put a finger to his lips and shook his head. "No more questions." He motioned for her to follow him back to the table. The recording had finished.

"I haven't heard that magnificent overture for years. Thank you for bringing it."

"Let me bring you up to date on your situation," said Jenkins. "You will be brought to trial for the crime of kidnapping a minor child who is a citizen of Ecuador. An American attorney has agreed to represent you. He consulted an official looking paper for the name. "Lorenzo Madrid. He has agreed to come to this country and appear in court with you. We hope for an acquittal, of course, or at least a lighter sentence than that prescribed by law."

"What kind of sentence is prescribed by law?" she asked.

Jenkins consulted his notes. "Ten years is the minimum."

The color drained from Maxine's face. "God, I can't survive another day in here, let alone another year or ten years."

"Let's take this one day at a time," continued Jenkins.

"Who will pay for this? I have no money."

"That I do not know. He has agreed to represent you, that's all I know at present. He is scheduled to arrive in three days."

Jenkins stood up and looked at his watch. "I've got several meetings back in Quito this afternoon so I have to go. I will keep you informed and bring Mr. Madrid up here to see you."

"The Ecuadorian government has agreed to let me be represented by an American attorney? That is wonderful, but seems odd to me."

"Not my decision, Ms. March."

They shook hands and he stood up. "How is your health?

"I have a cold and a bad cough most of the time," she said. She picked up his notepad and scrawled, "No medicine, not even aspirin!"

"How about the food? I don't imagine they feed you very well."

"Beans and rice and lots sardines. I hate those little creatures, although I guess they're protein."

"I'll lodge a complaint with the officials here on my way out. You need fresh fruit at the very least, and medicine."

"It can't be just for me," she said. "I've made friends with several women in here. They are helping me get through this. There needs to be enough for ten women, at least."

"I'll see what I can do," he said. "I don't want you to get your hopes up, Ms. March, but this is a good sign, I mean for the Ecuadorians to allow you to have an American lawyer. I'll keep you posted."

"Thank you, Mr. Jenkins. I appreciate what you're doing for me."

As soon as he had left the room, Gustavo entered by the rear door. "Good news, *Señorita* Marsh?"

"I'm going to trial and with an American attorney helping me."

"That is wonderful news," he said, guiding her to the door. "May I say, I enjoyed hearing your favorite piece of music." He winked and walked her down the long corridor and across the courtyard and into the building where her cell block was.

6

LORENZO SPENT THE NEXT DAY taking care of the hundreds of things he had to do before leaving for Ecuador, both business and personal. With Thad's help, Sam got continuances for two cases about to go before judges. He called both clients to explain his absence. Then he called his chief benefactor, Andrew Corning.

Lorenzo had gotten the young millionaire freed from a psychiatric clinic. His step-mother had committed him so she could take control of the lumber company that was rightfully his. When it became known that she had hired a hit man, first to scare Lorenzo off the case, then to kill him by various means, she had disappeared. The hit man had been shot after he tried to kidnap Tito. It was a long story, and one Lorenzo would just as soon forget.

In gratitude, Corning had put Lorenzo on a monthly retainer so he could call him for legal advice whenever he needed it. He also named him to the board of directors of Corning Timber Company.

"Andrew, it's Lorenzo. How are things going? Did you find someone to fill that superintendant's job at your Roseburg mill?"

Lorenzo listened. "Good. Say, Andrew, I wanted to let you know that I will be out of the country for a week beginning on Friday."

He listened. "It's a child custody case."

More listening. "No experience in foreign courts, but I'm hoping my brown skin and ability to speak Spanish will get me through," he laughed. "I'll be back in time for the quarterly board meeting. Let me know the issues you plan to deal with and if you need legal justification for anything."

They chatted for a few more minutes. "Okay, good. Great talking to you as always. I'll check in with you when I get back."

After getting Sam to research the Ecuadorian court system, Lorenzo left the building to get both a cholera and yellow fever shot. On the way out, he stuck his head in the door of the classroom. Both Tito and Jo looked up from the table where a board game was laid out.

"Hi, Papa. Miss Jo and I are studying whales, those great creatures from the sea. It's a game and it's fun."

"Good news, little man. I'll be back soon." The boy was so engrossed in the game that he barely looked up. Jo winked at Lorenzo and nodded her head.

"Did you know, Miss Jo, that the blue whale is the biggest creature on earth? But how can we say that since a whale does not walk on earth. He's only in the sea."

Lorenzo heard her reply as he closed the door.

"Well now, Master Tito, let's talk about why that is so."

As he did his errands, Lorenzo began to dread the evening when he would have to tell Tito that he was leaving him for a week.

✧ ✧ ✧ ✧ ✧

When he returned to the office after lunch, Lorenzo found Sam bent over a stack of pages strewn around the conference table. "I'm almost finished, boss. Give me a few and we can talk."

While he waited, he called his friend, Greg Nettles, from the DEA, who had helped him out of tight situations more than once. "Greg, how's my favorite secret agent?

"Lorenzo. You staying out of trouble?"

"Maybe yes, maybe no." He gave him a quick rundown on Maxine's arrest and his plan to defend her in court.

"You're going to do what? Where?" Lorenzo could hear the anger in his voice.

"Jesus H. Christ! You are crazy! You can't do it! You're putting your life in danger. You don't know Ecuador. You don't know the legal system there. You are crazier than I thought you were!"

"I've got to do it for Tito, Greg."

"What good will you be to him if you wind up in prison down there yourself?"

"Can you give me the names of any contacts there that I can call on in an emergency?"

"Hell, Lorenzo. This whole enterprise is an emergency, or will be!"

"Let's meet before I go, like tomorrow. You were stationed in South America for a while, right?"

"Yeah. Bolivia for two horrible years."

"Great. Tell me all. Tomorrow?"

"Shit. Why can't I ever refuse you! I owe you for Perez, I guess, but that's the only reason I'm doing this. Tell you what, I'm due for a few days off, and I was planning to go to the coast. How about I go through Corvallis and we have lunch? What's that place down by the Willamette?"

"Big River."

"Yeah. Meet you there at one, after the lunch crowd."

"And you'll give me a name or two?"

"Yeah, yeah, yeah!"

Lorenzo hung up the phone and looked over at Sam, who seemed to be finished with his research project. "Are you ready for me, Sam?"

"As you white folks say, ready as I'll ever be."

"But I'm not white, Sam," Lorenzo laughed.

"You are whole lot whiter than me, boss!"

EVEN THOUGH SAM LINCOLN HAD NO TRAINING OR EXPERIENCE as a legal researcher, he was a fast learner. "Okay, boss, please sit down at the table and I will lay out what I found out." For next hour, he did just that.

"The system of justice in Ecuador is carried out by five levels of what they call tribunals. What they call the parochial judge handles minor civil cases on the local level. Cantonal courts, one per canton, handle minor civil and some criminal action suits."

"What's a canton?"

"I was hoping you'd ask me that," Sam smiled. He pulled out a sheet of paper from the stack in front of him. "A canton is a small territorial district, like one of our counties."

"Got it!"

"Provincial courts take care of all but a few criminal cases and more serious civil suits. Superior courts handle appeals from cases in the lower courts. The Supreme Court has thirty-one justices chosen by the national assembly. Are you falling asleep, boss? I've got more to tell you."

"No, Sam, this is good stuff. Exactly what I need."

"My research tells me that the judicial system in Ecuador is subject to political pressure. Police officers are tried in closed session in special courts so abuse and other violations by the police are

rarely prosecuted. Even though there are laws against arbitrary arrest and detention, such violations occur." He looked up from his notes. "That was what happened to Maxine March, don't you think?"

"No doubt," said Lorenzo, shaking his head. "But how do I prove that?"

"That's why you're a good attorney and get paid the big bucks," he said, laughing.

"YEAH, RIGHT!"

"Some good news, maybe," Sam continued. "In 1998, a new Judicial Council was formed with the power to administer the court system and discipline judges. The first year after that, two judges were fired. But, according to my research, a lot of Ecuadorians mistrust the judicial system. That has resulted in people, in rural areas especially, taking the law into their own hands. That has led to the lynching and burning of suspects without trials."

"Not lawyers, though. Right?" laughed Lorenzo.

"What the hell are you getting yourself into, boss?"

"Yeah, I'm beginning to wonder. But I have to do it for Tito and for Maxine."

"One more thing: Ecuador is a signatory to something called the Hague Convention on the Protection of Children," continued Sam. "This means the law does not allow an Ecuadorian child to travel to the U.S. to be adopted. And let me read the official rule here: 'Therefore, prospective adoptive parents must obtain a full and final adoption under Ecuadoran law before the child can emigrate to the United States.'"

Sam looked up. "That means Maxine is screwed, boss. Don't you think?"

Lorenzo shook his head. "Maybe, but I have to try to help her, for Tito's sake if not Maxine's. As you recall, Paul Bickford is the one who actually took the boy from Ecuador, to save his life, I think. And he delivered him to her in the U.S."

"Can you get him to testify to that?"

"I'd like to try, but I don't know where he is. He's a Special Ops guy who goes from one trouble spot to the next, always in secret. His is a world of secrecy. She probably hasn't seen him for a year or so. My friend Tom Martindale told me that the two were a couple for only a brief time but Bickford could not commit to a long-term relationship. He gave her the kid and then vanished. I have no idea where he is or how to find him."

Sam shook his head, a sad look on his face. "I hope this helps," he said.

"Yes, a lot. I'll do my own research and talk to Thad Sampson. He mentioned that he knows someone here in Oregon who practiced law briefly in Ecuador or Peru or one of the countries in South America. I guess I should figure out the difference. Lots to do."

"I'll leave you to it, boss."

"Thank you, Sam. I hope you know I really value all you do for me."

Lorenzo spent the next two days learning all he could about the law in Ecuador, and specifically, the laws regarding foreign adoption and kidnapping. He feared that Maxine March's cause was hopeless if that charge stuck.

He had given Thad Sampson a list of his pending cases and their status. Sam would meet with him tomorrow in Salem for further instructions. He thought the entire list could be handled in a series of letters to the judges involved.

That night after dinner, Lorenzo decided he had put off telling Tito about his trip long enough. After Tito helped him clear the table, as he had insisted on doing lately, he led him into the living room. He sat down in a chair and pulled the boy over to him. Tito seemed to sense that something important was about to happen. He looked directly at Lorenzo with his big brown eyes.

"Papa? Is something wrong? You look sad."

Lorenzo pulled him close and kissed him on the top of his head. "Tito, I have to go on a trip."

"Can I go? Is it to the zoo or the lighthouse on the ocean?"

Lorenzo smiled. "Not this time but we will do that soon. When I get back. I promise."

The boy's eyes sparkled. "I would love that very much."

"I have to go on a longer trip and I'm afraid you have to say here with Sam and Miss Jo."

"Do I have to stay in their houses?"

"Do you want to do that?"

"Well, maybe not. I like this place very much. My room is here and all my books and toys."

"Okay. I thought you'd say that. That way your routine . . ."

"What is 'routine,' papa?"

"How you do things every day. Get up, eat breakfast, go to school, come home from school, have dinner, go to bed."

"And don't forget playing," he said, smiling.

"Yes, of course, playing—and how about getting tickled?"

Lorenzo rose and started whirling the boy around. When he sat him down, he started tickling him and then led him into his room to get ready for bed. "Okay, big guy, you need to take a bath. No one likes a stinky kid." Lorenzo filled the tub. As he had lately started to do on his own, Tito took off his clothes and stepped into the water. Lorenzo handed him a bar of soap and left the room.

"I'll be back," he said gruffly using an Arnold Schwarzenegger accent, the humor of which was probably lost on a boy who might never have seen the movie or any other in a theater or anywhere else.

Lorenzo turned down the covers as Tito walked into the room pulling on his Star Trek pajamas. "Wait a minute, buddy. You're still wet. Take off your shirt and I'll dry you off."

That done, he watched the boy climb into bed. "You're getting to be big," he smiled. "Remember, only a few weeks ago, I had to lift you into your bed. Now you do it on your own."

As he said that, tears formed in Lorenzo's eyes. He wiped them away. Tito didn't seem to notice and yawned.

"You are sleepy, I think. Too sleepy for a story. Right?"

"I guess so, papa. Will you be here when I wake up?"

"Of course. I will take you to the office and your school, and Miss Jo and Sam will be there waiting for you. Okay?"

"Okay. *Buenas noches, Papa.*"

"*Buenos noches, niño.*"

Lorenzo turned off all but a nightlight and closed the door to the boy's room. He was amazed at Tito's resilience.

He packed one bag with warm weather shirts and pants and a good suit and expensive shirt and ties—his court clothes. He also organized the research materials he needed to study on the flight. He made sure his passport, credit cards, and cash were on the dresser, ready to put into his pocket in the morning.

As he was undressing, he heard a soft knock on the front door. Unannounced callers were rare, but he had suspected he would get a visitor. He opened it cautiously to find a young Army officer. "Mr. Madrid? These documents are for you. I was told you were expecting them and that you would know how to proceed from here."

"Yes, captain, I do. I was told to expect you. Thank you."

He figured any questions would go without answers. If this officer knew anything, he would not be able to tell him. The young man saluted and walked back to an unmarked car, its motor idling at the curb. It quickly drove away as Lorenzo closed the door and locked it.

Inside the large manila envelope was everything Kurt Jenkins had told him about: plane tickets, a visa for Ecuador, a reservation at the Marriott Hotel, a map of Quito, details on how to get to the embassy, the name of his contact, who would meet his plane, plus $10,000 in cash, with a Post-it note that read "country uses U.S. dollar."

◻ ◻ ◻ ◻ ◻

Tito was very quiet during breakfast and on the ride to the office. Lorenzo assumed that the impending change was on his mind so he didn't say much to him. He parked the car on the street in front of the building and opened the door for the boy who quickly ran up the stairs. Both Jo and Sam were waiting for them in the hallway.

Tito ran to Jo and grabbed her around her legs. "Miss Jo, Miss Jo," he wailed. "My papa is leaving us."

Lorenzo walked over to Sam and Jo and hugged them. "I won't ever be able to repay you. I'll be in touch. Call Thad with any problems." Then he knelt down and pulled Tito to him.

"Okay, little man, I'm leaving you in charge. You are the boss while I am gone. Okay? Can you be strong for all of us? Sam and Jo will be with you always, both here and at our house. Okay? Be strong."

"Yes, Papa," said Tito, between sniffles.

Lorenzo turned and walked quickly down the hall, tears in his eyes.

◘ ◘ ◘ ◘ ◘

Given the lack of time, Lorenzo had called Greg Nettles the day before to switch their meeting to Salem while on his way to the Portland airport, and for coffee instead of lunch. They met at a Starbucks downtown.

"Like I said on the phone, you are one crazy guy to do this!"

"I know I am, but I've got to do this, for Tito if not Maxine."

Nettles handed him a folded piece of paper. "The names of guys you can call in an emergency. This kind of shit is not in their job descriptions. I told them about you and how you had helped us with Perez. They work out of an office in the embassy. Better to keep them out of it except for an emergency. The diplomats look down on working stiffs like us. All their striped-pants bull shit. They don't deign to even speak to our guys unless they need us."

"Got it," said Lorenzo, standing up. "I'll be there a week and I'll let you know how it went when I get back."

"You're going to do all of this—get her out of prison and out of the country—in a week?"

"That's for later. I'm just going to see what I'm facing."

"You're facing a world of hurt, that's what you're facing. And maybe a jail cell."

They embraced and Greg patted Lorenzo on the back. "Until we meet again, my friend. Godspeed."

"I didn't know you were religious, Greg," Lorenzo smiled.

"Only when I need to do a serious intervention, like now."

8

LORENZO'S FLIGHT FROM PORTLAND TO LOS ANGELES WAS TYPICAL— a crowded plane, seats so close together there was barely room to do more than squeeze in, indifferent service, no food, and a mother with a crying baby in the middle seat beside him. He'd brought his earphones, which blocked some of the sound. Later, the baby would spit up its food, some of which landed on his shirt sleeve. Fortunately, the flight only lasted two hours.

In L.A. he walked to the International Terminal and found the counter for LATAM Airlines, a South American company that had been recommended to him.

"*Buenas tardes, señor,*" said the beautiful young woman behind the counter. "You are returning home to Ecuador?"

"No, just going there on business," he said.

"Are you an actor?"

"Oh no, just a lawyer."

She blushed. "I am sorry. It is just that you look . . ."

Women and men both were often impressed by his good looks and reacted accordingly. Most of his life, at least in big cities, he had frequently been propositioned by both sexes.

"Just a lawyer," he repeated.

"Have a pleasant flight."

He walked to the gate, joining about fifty other people waiting to board the plane. The group was a mix of older vacationers in shorts and sweatshirts and Trump ball caps—no doubt headed for cruise ships—well-dressed business men and women, young mothers with children, and younger men and women dressed for a night of club hopping. The men were a bit too handsome and the women a bit too pretty to be real. It seemed to Lorenzo that they had to be actors or models headed for home or for an on-location photo shoot.

Lorenzo had paid extra for a seat in business class. Because it would be a long, ten hour flight, it was worth the extra cost to get the leg room, the better food, amenities like a wide choice of movies, and the good service.

As soon as he sat down, a male steward was at his side. *"Buenas tardes, Señor Madrid.* I am Alejandro Panza, Alex for short. I will be taking care of you on this flight. Please let me know if you need anything. Here is a copy of the *New York Times* and *The Economist*. Dinner will be served in one hour. Can I bring you a mixed drink or a glass of wine?"

"A gin and tonic, *por favor,* Alex."

"A good drink to prepare one's system for the tropics." Lorenzo had not noticed the fashionably dressed older woman seated next to him until she spoke. The seats were arranged two by two on the left and right side of the plane, plus two in each row of the center section. He had counted 24 people in business class. His seat mate was not all that close, a console separated them. "Margarita Acosta," she said, extending a bejeweled hand. "My friends call me Margo."

Lorenzo kissed her hand. "Lorenzo Madrid."

"I love a man who knows that chivalry and politeness are not dead. With that and your dark, good looks, I knew you were a Spanish gentleman the moment I saw you in the boarding area."

"Spanish, no, if you mean from Spain," he said. "Thank you, Alex." The steward placed his drink on the console.

"Señora Acosta? What can I bring for you?"

"A very dry martini, straight up. Bombay gin."

"*Sí, Señora Acosta.*"

"I always try to book my fights to and from my country when I know Alex is working. He is the son of an old classmate of mine. Very good family, impeccable manners. So what do you do, Mr. Madrid?"

Given the nature of his visit, a white lie was called for. He didn't know this woman. Although she looked like a rich and harmless socialite, he had learned a long time never to reveal anything to strangers. "I'm an attorney with a big firm in L.A. and we're looking to expand our client list to other countries. This is just an exploratory visit for me. Only a week."

"Interesting. Where will you be staying?"

"The Marriott."

"A good hotel, but not a great hotel," she said. "I know several others with better amenities and better food."

"It will be fine. I'm only here for a few days."

Lorenzo decided he had offered enough information about himself to his new acquaintance, Ms. Acosta. "What about you, *señora*? I've talked too much about myself.

"There is not much to tell," she said. "I come from a modest background. My father was an accountant. My mother was an artist of sorts who quit painting after my sister and I were born."

"Forgive me, *señora,* but you do not look like you are someone from modest means today."

She laughed. "I guess not. You see, I married well. To a foreign service officer in my country's diplomatic corps. He was once considered a candidate for foreign minister by a long ago president. Countries in Latin American do change presidents a lot, as you may have noticed."

"He is now retired?"

"No, he is dead. We were separated at the time after I caught him in bed with one of his male aides."

"Sorry, I didn't mean to pry."

"It is of no concern to me," she said with bitterness in her voice. "He was dead to me as soon as I opened the door of our bedroom and found him with Gaspar, a beautiful young man who I had even fancied for myself."

This was getting way too personal for Lorenzo. "So good to chat, *señora*. I think I need to close my eyes for a while. I've had some hectic days getting ready for this trip and, I expect, some more hectic days ahead."

"Of course. I might do the same."

Both turned off the lights over their seats. Lorenzo reclined his seat and pulled a blanket over himself.

"Shall I wake you for dinner, *señor?*" Alex was standing by the side of his seat.

"How soon?"

"One hour, sir."

"Wake me when it's ready. I am hungry and wouldn't want to miss dinner."

"As you wish."

In one hour, Alex was good to his word. "Here is a hot towel for your face and your dinner will be right along."

"I'll go to the bathroom and then be ready for that dinner."

He got up and made his way to one of the bathrooms. There were two of them at the front of the cabin. As he returned, he noticed through a half-closed curtain that the economy section was jammed with people. Every seat seemed full and he heard the din of voices and a crying baby or two. He felt relieved not to be back there.

As Lorenzo reached his seat, Alex was standing there with dinner on a tray covered with a linen napkin. He pulled off the covering to reveal a large steak, baked potato, a salad and a basket of bread.

"Red wine or white, Mr. Madrid?"

"White, please, Alex. Red wine gives me a headache."

"We can't have that now, can we?" said *Señora* Acosta. "Alex,

I'd like another martini and dinner when you get to it."

"*Sí, señora.*"

Her dinner and cocktail were served and they spent the meal making small talk. After dessert, she got up. "I need to stretch my legs. Sitting so long is not good for older people, at least that's what my doctor tells me."

When she returned, they spent the rest of the flight reading, eating more meals, and watching movies. In the eighth hour, Lorenzo got up and walked around the cabin ten times and to the bathroom before returning to his seat.

"I see you followed my advice, Lorenzo. May I call you that?"

"Of course."

"You may call me Margo."

"Thank you, Margo."

More small talk in the last hour of the flight. Alex returned with Lorenzo's coat, and Lorenzo tipped him generously. "You've made the flight very pleasant," he told Alex. "*Muchas gracias.*"

After they had landed and were gathering their belongs in preparation for leaving the plane, Margo handed him her card. "If you want a private tour of Quito while you are here—I mean, if you need a break from the tedious business of looking for new law clients—call me. I would love to have you to dinner."

"That is very kind," he said. "I might take you up on that offer."

"Please do, and I mean it. Also, I might add that, because of my husband's long service in various governments here, I have many connections. Good connections with people that I would be happy to introduce you to. I mean introductions to the right person can help someone in your situation a lot."

Suddenly, Margo Acosta's friendship took on a whole new dimension. "I can promise you I will call."

He followed her out of the plane, pausing to pick up her mink coat when it fell to the floor at one point. As they approached the customs and immigration area, a man in a chauffeur's uniform signaled to her and spoke to one of the guards standing at the exit gate. He tipped his hat and opened the gate for her.

"Chao," she said over her shoulder. "See you soon."

As Lorenzo turned towards the immigration desk, he saw a young man standing just inside the gate holding a sign that read "LORENZO MADRID." He walked over to him. "You must be Alberto Dragón."

"*Sí, señor.* I am that man. Please place the accent on the last syllable. I am definitely not a dragon! If you will give me your baggage ticket, I will fetch that bag and we can go to the car. When he returned, he flashed a card to the guard at the gate who opened it and they walked through.

"Welcome to Quito, Mr. Madrid," he said. "It is a big pleasure to meet you."

"And for me as well," said Lorenzo.

Because Alberto Dragón was obviously efficient and very good looking, Lorenzo decided his week in Ecuador would not be all that bad.

9

"TIME TO GET UP, SLEEPING BEAUTY," said Dawn. She and Sandra stood over Maxine's cot.

Maxine stirred. "What time is it?"

"The usual. 5 a.m.," said Sandra. "Let's get you up. How are you feeling this morning?"

"Better, I think." She felt her head. "No temperature. I mean my forehead doesn't feel hot."

Dawn touched it, nodded her head, and they pulled Maxine to her feet. "You got to at least go through the motions in the laundry today, sick or not. You don't want to give them any reason to call off the visit with your lawyer."

"When's he comin'?" asked Sandra.

"Tomorrow. The guy from the embassy is bringing him here."

Both of them guided her gently to the shower. Sandra ordered the two women in there to get out, and they did, quickly. Her fearsome reputation followed her everywhere in the prison. No one wanted to get on the bad side of "Big Sandra," as she was known.

After eating breakfast, the three walked to the laundry and went to work. At noon, when they broke for their meager lunch meal, Gustavo walked by and dropped a piece of paper on the floor at Maxine's feet.

**Visit with lawyer set. Pick up you
at 2 in afternoon, take to visitor
area or maybe front office.
Excuse bad ingles.**

Maxine smiled, hid both hands under the table and then tore the note into tiny pieces, which she swallowed with a gulp of foul-tasting coffee.

"All set," she whispered to the two of them. "Tomorrow at 2."

By the end of the day, Maxine's spirits rose. The prison pallor faded as she smiled and talked animatedly for the first time in weeks.

"You are lookin' good, girl," said Sandra as she patted her on the back. Lookin' very good."

The three of them spent the rest of the day putting together an outfit of decent looking clothes the two of them had scrounged from various sources—a skirt and blouse, a shawl, and leather shoes with heels that were just high enough to look stylish.

Just trying on the clothes made Maxine feel a whole lot better, even if the next day's meeting didn't result in her freedom.

10

ALBERTO LED LORENZO THROUGH THE LUXURIOUS LOBBY of the Marriott to the front desk. He placed Lorenzo's passport on the counter and rattled off several sentences in Spanish to the desk clerk in a stern tone that demanded attention. The beautiful young woman on duty looked startled but quickly brought up Lorenzo's reservation on her screen. "Are you *Señor* Madrid?" she said to Alberto.

He shook his head and stepped aside. "*Mi patrón está Señor Madrid.*"

She looked relieved when Lorenzo stepped to the counter and pulled his credit card out of his wallet. "*Gracias, Señorita . . .*" He looked at her name tag. "*Obrigón.*"

She activated his room card keys and handed them to him. "We hope you enjoy your stay, *señor*. The elevators are to your right. Your room is on the twelfth floor. While you are here, you might teach your assistant some manners."

Alberto's face turned red as she turned around abruptly and walked through a door to the back.

Lorenzo smiled as they walked to the elevators. "I don't think you impressed her with your approach," he laughed. "Whatever you were attempting to do, it didn't work!"

Alberto shook his head, a sad look on his face. "I know, I know, *patrón*. Maybe you can give me some tips on how to

deal with the ladies."

Lorenzo didn't answer, but thought to himself that Alberto probably had more experience dealing with ladies than he did.

◘ ◘ ◘ ◘ ◘

After the two of them had lunch at the hotel, Alberto drove Lorenzo to the embassy.

Even though he had been gone from the U.S. for only a day, Lorenzo felt comforted when they drove through the gates. This was United States soil and the American flag fluttering in the breeze made him feel safe—from what, he did not know. The Marine guard directed them to a visitor parking area in front of an imposing building.

"This is called the chancellery," explained Alberto. "This is where the big shots hang out. Mr. Jenkins has his office here."

They walked into a spacious lobby with high glass walls at the far end and a desk and two rows of gates with metal detectors on either side. Another Marine guard was sitting at the desk.

'Hey, bro," said Alberto. "This is my buddy, Lorenzo."

He turned to Lorenzo. "This is my buddy Sergeant Parks. Me and him go way back."

The Black sergeant and Lorenzo shook hands. "Let me find you in the appointment list." He scanned a typewritten page. "Here you are. To see Mr. Jenkins."

"Yes," said Lorenzo. "Kurt Jenkins."

"Please clip this visitor's badge on your coat and remove all metal objects from your pockets. If you've got a cell phone or any recording device, please put it in that tray before you go through the metal detector."

Lorenzo and Alberto walked to the gate where another Marine guard stood waiting for them. He was Hispanic.

"¡Qué tal!, Hugo? ¿Cómo está?"

"Muy bien. Please step through the gate, sir."

Lorenzo did that, followed by Alberto.

"Hugo's from California, Lorenzo. Aren't you from there?"

"I used to he. Where in California?"

"South Central L.A."

"East L.A."

"Wow, sir. A small world. Enjoy your visit here." He turned toward the approaching figure of an older American woman, who ignored the two others and extended her hand towards Lorenzo. "Alice Dunkirk. Like the World War II battle."

"Lorenzo Madrid, like the city in Spain."

They both laughed.

"A beautiful place Madrid. I was posted there for five years. If you'll follow me, I'll take you to Mr. Jenkins. He is waiting for us."

Lorenzo turned toward Alberto.

"They don't let me upstairs too often, Mr. Madrid," he laughed.

Ms. Dunkirk nodded slightly as if she agreed with the policy of keeping the underlings in their places.

"See you in a bit, then? You'll wait here?" asked Lorenzo.

"You bet I will, boss. I'll just pass the time with my friend Sergeant Parks until you get back."

Ms. Dunkirk led Lorenzo up a beautiful angular staircase that belonged in a Busby Berkeley musical from the 1930s, only then there would be beautiful dancing girls in sweeping ball gowns. He figured that only Dunkirk would know what he was talking about. There are some advantages to being older.

"You're smiling, Mr. Madrid," she said when they reached the second floor.

"I was thinking that the grand staircase belonged in a Busby Berkeley musical from the 1930s."

"A what?" she asked, a perplexed look on her face.

"Oh nothing. I was thinking of an old movie I once saw."

"Oh, yes, I see. Here we are at Mr. Jenkins's office. He's waiting for us."

She escorted him into a large and ornate room dominated by a map of Ecuador that covered half of a wall and an American flag by the side of a desk. The other walls were covered floor-to-ceiling with bookshelves.

Jenkins got up and walked to Lorenzo, his hand extended. "Good to meet you at last," he said, shaking Lorenzo's hand vigorously.

"Good to meet you as well, sir."

"Please call me Kurt."

He turned to Ms. Dunkirk. "Please hold my calls, Alice. And have Elena bring us some coffee."

Jenkins motioned for Lorenzo to sit in one of the four chairs pulled in a semi-circle around the fireplace. "You'll love the coffee. It's from across the border in Colombia. Remember those old commercials featuring Juan Valdez? They roast great beans there still, although in recent years, Colombia has been known more for cocaine than coffee."

They sat down, and soon a young Hispanic woman entered the room carrying a tray holding a large coffee pot, two cups and saucers, and a plate of cookies. The young woman filled two cups and left the room.

"*Muchas gracias, Lena.*"

After the door closed, Jenkins leaned closer to Lorenzo. "You notice I didn't ask Alice to get the coffee. She is a stickler for protocol. Fetching coffee would be way below her concept of her job description. She's a great executive assistant, though, so I'm not complaining."

The two sipped coffee for a few minutes and then Jenkins broke the silence.

"Good of you to come, Mr. Madrid. Ms. March speaks highly of you. She said you were the only one who could help her. Can you fill me in on why she said that?"

Lorenzo was wary of revealing too much about the Maxine/Tito situation lest the information be revealed to the wrong person. On the other hand, given his shaky status in Ecuador and Maxine's perilous situation, he had no choice. This was, after all, an official of that American government. "You know about the boy."

"Yes. Tito. He's living with you presently."

"Right. She left him with me when she came down here. He is seven and a great kid. I have hired a tutor for him and he is doing well in our little school. He's very smart."

"Is Paul Bickford the father?"

Lorenzo flinched at the mention of that name. "No. He's an orphan as far as we know."

"You seemed surprised that I mentioned Paul."

"I know his earlier involvement with both Maxine and the boy. He is the one who brought him to the U.S. in a U.S. military plane, I think. Maxine was out of Ecuador by then. I didn't realize that he was still around. She has never mentioned him to me and certainly didn't think of asking for his help now."

Jenkins picked up a folder from a small table and opened it. Lorenzo could see the words TOP SECRET emblazoned on the cover. He handed several pages to Lorenzo.

Even before Lorenzo started reading, Jenkins summarized the contents. "Bickford's a bit of a rogue agent, a loose cannon, if you will. He loves adventure and ignoring the rules. As an Army spook, he has gotten away with a great deal during his long military career. I gather he and Ms. March were once in love?"

"Probably," said Lorenzo, "but she and I have never discussed that."

"But she didn't call on him for help before she came to you."

"I'm sure she had no idea where to find him."

"Somehow he heard about her arrest here and her imprisonment, and he tried to get her out."

"Bickford was here?" said Lorenzo, a startled look on his face. "God, that's hard to believe!"

"Showed up early one morning a few weeks ago and tried to storm the place with a bunch of guys from our embassy who do things like that all the time all over South America."

"The attempt failed, obviously, or I wouldn't be here trying to do the same thing legally now. What happened?" asked Lorenzo.

"Someone tipped off the prison authorities and soldiers were waiting for our guys when they got to the prison. They opened fire and everyone was killed."

Lorenzo shook his head. "Including Bickford?"

Jenkins pulled another page out of the folder and handed it to Lorenzo. "That's what we thought. The soldiers waited until daybreak to clear the bodies away, but when they showed up, they found only a few shell casings on the jungle floor, and a lot of bloody clothing."

"Bickford's?"

Jenkins shrugged. "He's a spook, you know, an expert at faking his own death and disappearing. We only got fragmentary reports in the days after. Those guys never reveal much of anything to anyone, and certainly not to what they consider a bunch of candy-assed, striped-pants diplomats."

"So he may or may not be dead. Does Maxine know about any of this?"

"No, I didn't tell her. I think she'd be crushed by knowing about his death and also by the fact that he might have gotten her out."

"Yeah, you're right," said Lorenzo. "Too bad in many ways, not the least of which is the fact that I could use some of his der-ring-do in the days ahead."

Jenkins filled their cups with more coffee and then handed Lorenzo another page from his folder. As before, he summarized it before Lorenzo could read it himself. "The following morning, one of our local informants reported hearing the whirring sound of a helicopter motor near his post in the jungle. He ran to the edge of a clearing and saw a small aircraft land and two men stagger out of the brush, dragging a third. The crew rushed to help them and they all climbed aboard."

Lorenzo scanned the page. "This says they were taken to a medical facility in Panama and then on to an Army hospital in

Texas."

"That's all we knew. Calls to that hospital by the ambassador and even an assistant secretary in D.C. were not answered. Not even a 'confirm or deny' statement."

"So we don't know if Bickford died there or survived?"

Jenkins nodded. "Until last week, the day before I called you."

Jenkins pulled another page out of the folder and handed it to Lorenzo. "This is a copy of some kind of bank draft?"

"Yeah, for $50,000. And it had a note attached to it."

Lorenzo read the few words scrawled on it.

Call Lorenzo Madrid in Oregon. Use this money to get her out of that hell hole. P.B.

11

AFTER LORENZO LEFT, Jo and Sam made sure that Tito's life went on as it always had. That attempt at normalcy was hard because of one fact: Lorenzo, who had been his protector and constant companion for a year, was gone.

The little boy was his usual buoyant self most days. He worked hard on his lessons with Jo and talked easily with her and Sam in the evenings. But there were times when he revealed his real feelings. One night, after Jo had put him to bed, she heard sobs coming from his room. She opened the door and found him crouched on the floor by his bed rocking back and forth, his little arms tight around his body.

"What is this, little darlin'?" she said, crossing the room, picking him up, and then sitting on the bed with him in her lap. "What's wrong?"

"My papa has left me and is never coming back," he wailed. "I don't know what I did to make him go away from me."

"Oh no, Tito, he is just on a trip he had to make," she said. "He loves you very much. He had to make the trip because of you. I know that for a fact."

Tito looked at Jo, his voice quaking and tears running down his face. "He does? He really does?"

"Yes! Would I ever lie to you?"

"No, I guess not," he said, wiping his eyes with his hand.

"Here, use this," she said, handing

him a handkerchief. "And blow your nose. We don't want any snot running down that beautiful face, now do we?"

"No, I guess not," he said.

"What's going on in here with you two," said Sam standing in the doorway wearing some kind of weird looking nightshirt.

"Saints preserve us," said Jo. "Whatever are you wearing? It looks like something the cat dragged in."

"Say what?" said Sam, a smile on his face. "How dare you laugh at my nightshirt!"

He walked to the bed and swept Tito up in his arms, tickling him until the boy began to giggle. "That's more like it, Mr. Tito. No room for grumps in this house!" He set him down on the floor.

"That's much better, Tito," said Jo. "Who would like a nice cup of hot chocolate?"

"We do," yelled Tito and Sam at the same time.

As they walked into the kitchen, Tito looked up at Jo. "How could a cat drag in Sam's nightshirt, when we don't have a cat?"

"That's a fair point, Master Tito, a fair point."

▢ ▢ ▢ ▢ ▢

Outside, in a car parked across the street, two men lit cigarettes at the same time.

"How long do we just sit here doing nothing?" asked the younger one. "We need to take care of these people and get back to L.A. This is all bullshit and really boring."

"You need to be patient, Alfredo. We wait for the boss to tell us what to do. Besides, it will not serve any purpose to kill the boy and the old lady, or even the Black man. We need to wait for the *jefe* to return from wherever he went. He'll be back and then we will get them."

The older man drew a finger across his throat in an imaginary thrust. Then the two of them broke into laughter.

12

EARLY THE NEXT MORNING, Dragón picked Lorenzo up at the hotel and drove him to the Embassy. Jenkins was standing next to an official looking car parked in the driveway, motor running, rear door open. "You've got a free day, Alberto," he said to the young man. "Be back here by five, *por favor.*"

"*Sí, señor.* Have a pleasant journey to wherever you are going."

"Not sure I mentioned that we will be flying to Guayaquil," said Jenkins as the car pulled away. "It's too far to drive."

"I didn't realize that this case had that much of a high profile," said Lorenzo.

"Maybe not at home, but it has been big news down here."

"Is that good news or bad news?" asked Lorenzo.

"Maybe the latter," said Jenkins. "Some leftist politicians have used it to rally their supporters—American woman kidnaps poor Ecuadorian orphan. That kind of thing."

"Yes, of course. That is understandable. We are the ugly Americans wherever we go, especially now with our idiotic president."

"I didn't hear that!" said Jenkins. "Diplomats are neutral."

"But they must have opinions."

"Opinions they keep to themselves," said Jenkins, a smile on his face.

"We are at the airport."

The driver drove the car through a

gate marked *DIPLOMÁTICO SOLAMENTE!* He stopped the car at a small jet plane with U.S. Air Force markings on the tail. A tall Air Force sergeant opened the door.

"Thank you, sergeant."

"You gentlemen can go right up the stairway."

They mounted the stairs and were greeted by another Air Force sergeant, this one a woman. "Welcome, gentlemen," she said. "Please sit down in those seats up front. "I'll bring coffee and breakfast as soon as we are airborne. We're waiting for two other passengers."

Lorenzo and Jenkins took seats in the second row and buckled up. "I am amazed that this is all so official," said Lorenzo in a low voice. "I mean the military plane and the personal interest you obviously have in this case."

"There are several reasons, two official, the other practical," he said. "This has become a *cause célèbre* here in Ecuador. 'American woman kidnaps Ecuadorian boy,' as I've said. Also, you are well-known in law enforcement circles as the guy who helped bring down a drug lord because of your cooperation with the DEA a few years back."

"And the practical?"

"Guayaquil's too far to drive and return in one day."

"Makes sense," said Lorenzo, shrugging his shoulders.

"So the prison authorities know all about my visit with Maxine March?"

"Oh yes. The head of the prison system authorized it."

"Why so cooperative if she is viewed as a notorious kidnapper?"

"Politics has played a role here. The new president of Ecuador needs American aid and private investment in order to pay for a lot of ambitious and costly new programs. While he can't be seen to go too easy on her, he seems committed to see that she gets a fair trial."

"So there will definitely be a trial."

"Yeah, I can't see any way to avoid it. But that's where you come in. You're Hispanic and well-known and cut an imposing figure."

Lorenzo laughed. "Not sure how imposing I'll be in a strange courtroom in a country I know little about."

Just then, they turned to watch the last two passengers board the plane and walk down the aisle towards them. The four shook hands and the shorter of the two leaned over and whispered in Lorenzo's ear. "We're DEA. Greg Nettles sent us to watch your back."

◻ ◻ ◻ ◻ ◻

As soon as the plane landed, it taxied to a small building away from the main terminal. They disembarked even before the engines had been turned off.

An unmarked car was waiting for them at the end of the airplane stairway. It was not the sleek embassy car that took them to the airport in Quito but a decrepit taxi. No one opened the doors as they piled in the back. "Sorry, sir," said the driver, a dark-skinned Hispanic who needed a shave. "It's best not to flaunt our nationality around here. "Herman Soto."

The three shook hands. "I'll drive you to the prison. It's just outside of town."

They drove in silence for the first few miles, then Jenkins pulled a sheet of paper from his briefcase and began reading from it. "The Guayaquil prison—formally called Litoral—is the largest in the country. There are two sections. The male prison holds about 1,100 men and the female prison about 300 or so, plus sixty children."

"Kids in a prison?" said Lorenzo, a startled look on his face.

"With their mothers inside, they have no place to go. Most of the women are in there for non-violent crimes. About twenty percent of them are there on drug-related charges. The men and women are in separate sections, of course. Bribes are the key to survival. You need to pay for better food and clothes and to hire a

54

lawyer. If you don't pay, you are thrown into Pavilion Three, which is dirty and infested with rats the size of rabbits and roaches and God knows what else. The food there is horrible too, mostly rice and sardines. Things only get better if you offer bribes, I presume to guards and maybe even officials."

"God, what a nightmare!" said Lorenzo.

"Ms. March got lucky. She told me that two American women started helping her as soon as she got there. Dawn Young and someone called Sandra, last name unknown. They gave her clothes and better food. She did run afoul of some prison official who was passing through and took a dislike to her because of the kidnapping charge. As a result she was moved to Pavilion Three until that official left and she was moved back to her old area. Unfortunately, the bad conditions impacted her health. She is not well, Lorenzo. The medical care in there is spotty. She was coughing repeatedly when I saw her and had lost a lot of weight. The longer she stays in there, the worse it will be for her. We've got to get her out somehow."

At that point, the car stopped at what appeared to be the main gate of the prison. Soto flashed a card, the metal barrier rose slowly and creakily, and the taxi drove through. From inside, the prison did not look as formidable as it apparently was. The administration building was a two story structure that could have housed a school in the U.S. with a lawn and some flower beds in the front. Someone was even mowing the grass. "Not as bad as I expected," muttered Lorenzo.

"Like a movie set, I'm afraid, or a Potemkin Village," said Jenkins. "Look over there."

Lorenzo glanced at another, higher gate to the right just as it opened to allow a truck to drive out. Two-story buildings lined the road. All the windows had bars on them and hands sticking out, most holding cigarettes.

"No glass?" said Lorenzo. "Must get pretty cold inside."

"You got it, sir," said Soto from the front seat.

As the gate closed, one of the men must have caught sight of their car and them. First one, then many more started whistling and shouting at them.

Soto turned toward Jenkins and Lorenzo. "These guys see two good-looking men and they go nuts," he laughed, shaking his head. "They're pretty horny."

Jenkins shuddered as if he had a chill. "We wouldn't last five minutes in there," he said.

"Try five seconds," said Soto. He stopped the car in front of a main door. An older fat man and a younger looking guard were standing outside. The guard opened the door and Lorenzo and Jenkins got out.

"Guillermo Del Rey at your service," said the fat man, clicking his heels together and bowing. "I am the governor of the Litoral Nationál Prisión, the finest in the sovereign nation of Ecuador."

"Lorenzo Madrid." They shook hands.

"Kurt Jenkins, second secretary of the United States Embassy here in Ecuador."

Del Ray turned to the younger man standing beside him. "This is Gustavo Montez. He is the one in charge of the unit where *Señorita* March is housed."

Montez stepped forward and shook their hands. "*Mucho gusto, señores.*"

"Gustavo will be at your service while you are here in my prison," said Del Rey. "He will take you to *Señorita* March. I have arranged for you to speak in a special place. Gustavo."

As the warden or governor or whatever he was called, walked away, Montez motioned for them to follow him. They entered a lobby area and turned to the left, down a short hall, through a door and into a small room, which contained a sofa and a table with four chairs. "Please sit," he said. "I will get the *señorita.*"

"A real contrast to what we just saw," whispered Lorenzo.

Before he could comment, the door opened and Maxine rushed in, tears running down her face. "Lorenzo, Lorenzo," she sobbed. "I never thought I'd see you again!"

They embraced as Jenkins stood by awkwardly. She turned toward to diplomat. "Mr. Jenkins. I need to hug you too."

She looked at Gustavo, a frightened look on her face as if she had broken a rule she would be punished for later. "Is this permitted? I mean to touch someone in this manner?"

"Do not worry, *señorita*. This has all been arranged by the governor himself."

Maxine hugged Jenkins, who stood stiffly at first, but then relaxed. "I owe you both so much," she said.

Gustavo was smiling. "I will be outside so you can have some privacy for your legal conference." He left the room.

After he was gone, Jenkins pointed to a large chandelier hanging above the table as if to warn that it might have a microphone hidden in its elaborate crystal designs. Both Maxine and Lorenzo nodded.

"First of all, I want to ask how my family is doing in the U.S.," she said. "How is my little nephew?"

Lorenzo pulled a small photo of Tito out of his pocket and handed it to her. Tears filled her eyes as she held the photo tightly and then kissed it. "My, he has certainly grown into a big boy."

She mouthed the words "thank you."

"Your sister says he is doing well in school. He is very smart."

"Does he go to public school?"

"No, your sister decided to hire a tutor and she has set up a regular school room near her office."

"That is good news," said Maxine, her eyes again filling with tears. "Please give her my best wishes and my nephew too."

"I will do that," said Lorenzo, handing her a handkerchief.

She dabbed at her eyes and blew her nose.

"How is your health?" asked Lorenzo. "Do you get any kind . . ."

"It is such a nice day, why don't we step into the garden for a few moments?" interrupted Jenkins, who pointed to a door that opened to the outside.

The three walked outside. "We need to make this fast," said Jenkins. "Here's the plan, Maxine. Early next week, I think, you will be moved to a small jail in the court building in Quito for the preliminary hearing. You will be formally charged and Lorenzo will enter a plea for you. You should not say anything at that time. I can't emphasize that enough. You recall the case of Lori Berenson in Peru in the nineties?"

Both Maxine and Lorenzo nodded.

"Her frequent outbursts in the courtroom hurt her case a lot. Any chance at leniency was forgotten because she was so unpleasant."

"I will be quiet as a mouse."

"Glad you understand. I'll hold you to that," said Jenkins.

Lorenzo turned to Maxine. "We were asking about your health. How are you feeling? You look very tired."

"Some days are better than others," she said. "I do have a cough and a fever from time to time, but there's no chance of seeing a doctor. You'd have to be half dead—or dead. My friends in here can get some medications and they give me some other stuff that helps. God knows what it is, but if it makes me feel better, I take it."

She turned to Lorenzo. "Enough about my health. You mentioned the hearing and then what?"

"Before the hearing, I intend to go to Montecristi for a look at the scene of your supposed crime," said Lorenzo. "I want to retrace your steps and try to find out more information about Tito and his family."

"I had found some letters and photos in an old trunk just before the police arrested me," she said. "I'm not sure where they are. Maybe the rich woman whom I met on the bus has them."

"Do you recall her name?"

Maxine shook her head. "That day was a nightmare and I guess my mind is shutting it out."

"No problem," said Lorenzo. "I'll see if I can locate her while I'm there."

"Be careful, Lorenzo. She is the one who called the authorities. She had me arrested."

"Did you see her again?" asked Jenkins.

"No."

"I'll get back the day before your hearing so I can represent you competently, with all the facts I can find."

She turned to Jenkins. "Do I have any chance at all of getting out of this place? This garden is lovely but it's all a show for your benefit."

"Keep your voice down. We need to show how much we appreciate their courtesy. I doubt any of the American women who are in here with you would get this kind of treatment."

"Why me?" she asked.

"Two factors. One, you are intelligent and obviously not a drug addict or someone who smuggled drugs for your boyfriend. Two, Lorenzo, a fellow Latino, is your attorney. He will cut a striking figure in the courtroom, handsome like a matinee idol in one of the Mexican movies so many people down here watch all the time."

Lorenzo looked uncomfortable. "Not sure about any of that. But I will do my best to represent you and get you out of here and back to the U.S. Take care of yourself."

Lorenzo could not quite bring himself to say the words I am sure Maxine was hoping to hear: "Back to your little boy, Tito."

Jenkins and Lorenzo walked back inside where Gustavo was waiting for her. Maxine looked back and waved to them as she disappeared into the black hole of the prison.

13

THE FLIGHT BACK TO QUITO WAS UNEVENTFUL. Alberto Dragón was waiting for them at the airport and escorted them to an embassy car. Both Lorenzo and Jenkins were tired from their long day so said little on the drive into the city.

"I'll drop you here, boss," said Alberto as he turned into the hotel driveway. "What time do you want to leave in the morning?"

"Come at seven, and I'll buy your breakfast."

As Lorenzo got out of the car, Jenkins touched his arm. "Be careful in Montecristi, Lorenzo. That's where Maxine got into trouble."

"I'll be there to watch his back," said Alberto from the front seat. "I'll be his bodyguard."

"Why doesn't that make me feel better," laughed Lorenzo. "I'm bigger than you, Alberto."

"But I'm young and strong. You'll distract the bad guys with your good looks and I'll clobber them in the meantime."

"Sounds like a recipe for total disaster," said Jenkins, a smile on his face. "I'll have a SWAT team ready."

The car drove away and Lorenzo walked into the lobby. As he disappeared through the door, one of two men sitting in a car parked a bit further down the driveway lit a cigarette. His companion punched in a number on a cell phone and listened. *"Buenas noches, señor.*

Americano está en hotél."

◻ ◻ ◻ ◻ ◻

After breakfast the next morning, Lorenzo and Alberto left the hotel in the decrepit taxi that belonged to the embassy.

"I really wanted my trip to be more luxurious than this," said Lorenzo from the back seat. "With the American flag on each fender flying in the breeze."

"You speak in jest. Right *señor?"*

"Yes, I'm kidding, Alberto. I'd be happy to sit up there with you so we can talk."

"I would like that, too, but I was instructed by *Señor* Jenkins that you need to be back there since this is supposed to be a taxi. Someone might be watching us."

"Yes, you're right, Alberto. Do you think the government cares enough about me to have security guys following me?"

"Oh yes, Lorenzo. I am sure of it. I haven't seen anyone following us, but they are around. This is a democratic country but the government always, how do you say, 'keeps an eye' on visitors. And the case of *Señorita* March is big news here. I mean, people don't like it when some *gringa* steals one of our kids."

"I understand, but the story is much more complicated than that. When it's all over, I'll tell you more."

They rode in silence for several more miles.

"Does it bother you to be involved in this, Alberto? I'll understand if you want me to ask Jenkins to replace you on this assignment."

"Oh no, sir. It is my job to help you. I like you, and I want to protect you. I will not betray you."

"Thank you, Alberto. I appreciate that. I trust you and feel safe with you."

Both of them fell silent for the last half hour of the trip.

◻ ◻ ◻ ◻ ◻

Montecristi was small—a modest cathedral was on one side of the central plaza and a hotel on the other. A few shops filled in around the square. Small houses had been built on all the streets, some paved, some only dirt. Alberto parked the car and they both walked around the plaza, which was filled with tables holding crafts, no doubt made by the women standing behind them. The predominant product was Panama hats.

Lorenzo looked quizzically at Alberto. "This isn't Panama."

"Very true, boss, but not many of those hats are made there any more. These ladies here and in homes all around this town spend all their time making these hats."

"I do remember Tito saying something about that, now that you mention it," said Lorenzo. "I guess I thought it was a little boy's exaggeration."

They strolled around the plaza for a time, with Lorenzo stopping to examine a small hat, ideal for Tito.

"Before we leave, I'll come back and get this one for my little . . . for Tito."

Alberto handed the hat to the woman in the stall. "*Vuelvo enseguida*," he told her. She smiled and put the hat into a bag and under her chair.

The two of them walked to another Catholic church on a street a block away from the plaza. It was small but impressive, with lovely stained glass windows and beautifully carved wooden doors.

Lorenzo had not been to church since he was a little boy. His mother made him and his sisters go to church in Boyle Heights, the neighborhood in Los Angeles where he grew up.

He walked down the center aisle, followed by a reluctant Alberto. Their shoes made tapping sounds on the tile floor as they walked. The air was filled with the fragrance of incense and flowers.

"Let's sit for a moment," Lorenzo whispered to Alberto as they slid into a pew a few rows from the altar. "You okay with this?"

he asked.

"I don't go to church much," said Alberto, shrugging his shoulders, "but I'm a good person."

"You don't have to go to church to be a good person, my son," said a voice from the side. A priest walked out from behind the altar with both arms extended.

"Welcome to our little church and our little town," he said, grasping their hands in his. "I am *Padre Castillo.*"

"Lorenzo Madrid," he said with a slight bow. "This is my friend Alberto Dragón." All three of them shook hands.

"What brings you here?" said the priest. *"Turistas?"*

"Not really, although I am enjoying your nice town." Lorenzo hesitated, then decided to run the risk of telling Castillo more. "I am looking for anyone who can give me information about a little boy I know in the United States. He is from this town."

Lorenzo pulled Tito's photo out of his wallet and handed it to Castillo. "Do you know this boy? Have you ever seen him before? He left here about a year ago."

Castillo studied the photo. "I've see this boy's photo before. Over a month ago. A nice American lady came here and asked me about him. I told her I knew a little bit about this boy. He lived with his grandmother in a shack a few blocks from here. His mother and father were dead. I have since found out that the grandma died too."

"Did the American lady say where she was going after she left you?

"No, but I imagine she was going to try to find that shack."

Lorenzo knew some of this but wanted to get the priest's version to see if he had more information that would help.

"That's what we'll do, too. *Gracias, padre.*"

"*Por nada.* That way," he said as they walked out of the church. He gestured up the hill. But then he motioned for them to come back. "I just thought of one more thing," he said. I might have something about the boy and his grandma and maybe his mother.

I have some records, ledgers really, of the names and other information about all the parishioners we have had. Let me look while you look for that place where they lived. Come back here when you have finished."

"Thank you, Father Castillo," said Lorenzo. "I would be most grateful."

Lorenzo and Alberto walked away and the priest walked back into the church. As soon as all three of them were out of sight, two men in dark suits followed the priest into the church.

14

THE MOMENT SAM, JO, AND TITO REACHED THE SECOND FLOOR of Lorenzo's office building, something seemed wrong. First, there was a smell—cigar smoke and cheap aftershave cologne. Then there was the door to the office. It was wide open with pieces of wood on the floor from the jimmied door frame.

"Take the boy back downstairs Jo, while I look around," said Sam. "I don't like the looks of this. Just go into a store and be around people."

"What's wrong?" said Tito, looking very worried. "Are bad men here?"

Jo picked him up and carried him back to the stairway. "No bad people are going to harm my baby boy!"

"I am not a baby!" protested Tito. "I am big!"

"Yes, you are, little man," said Sam. "Just go with Jo for a while. I'll come and get you after I look around. Okay?"

"Okay, Sam," said Tito, begrudgingly. "Let's go Jo. But put me down first!"

After the two of them were down the stairs, Sam walked into the classroom. With no weapon, he wouldn't be able to do much if someone were still there, except make a huge fuss. His mama had always said that he could out-shout all his brothers and sisters, and most anyone else.

Inside, the classroom seemed untouched. The books, games, and toys

Jo and Tito used each day were neatly in their proper places on shelves and in bins. He walked into the anteroom and stopped.

"Good God! What a mess!"

File drawers were open with papers strewn around on the floor. Books had been pulled from shelves and several of the smaller tables tipped over. The drawers in Lorenzo's desk were open, contents strewn around. Only the bottom drawer was closed. This was the part of his desk that Lorenzo had had custom made just in case this very thing happened. Although there were wood shavings on the floor in front of the desk, the drawer itself was closed. Lorenzo had told Sam when they were moving in that he had not had time to buy a safe but that this reinforced drawer would be a good substitute. Whatever was in there was safe, at least for now.

Sam needed to get Jo and Tito in the school room so he went downstairs. He found them in the paper store below looking at a rack of colored pencils and pens.

"Hey guys," he said. "What y'all doin'?"

"Sam, Sam. Look at all these colored pencils? I love them and here's nice paper with squares on each sheet. I can draw on them and the lines will help me keep things straight. Wish I had some."

"You little beggar," said Sam, who reached down to deliver a mock punch to Tito's chin.

"Tito always needs supplies," said Jo. "I'll buy them for you, Tito."

"Oh, Miss Jo," shouted Tito. "Thank you. I love you and Sam and my dad, Lorenzo."

Jo and Sam exchanged looks.

"Okay, guys," said Sam. "Let's pay for this stuff and then get to work. Your school should have started a long time ago."

"Yeah, but it's fun to hang around with you guys."

"Listen to you, little man.," said Sam, shaking his head. You are pickin' up American slang."

"Yes, I'm a big boy now and can talk like an American."

Upstairs, Jo started Tito on his lessons for the morning, being careful to keep him from the door that connected the schoolroom to the anteroom of Lorenzo's office.

It took Sam two hours to put the files back into the drawers. He'd have to sort them out later, relying on Lorenzo to recall what went with what.

He heard Jo and Tito talking all morning—multiplication tables and something about centipedes from the sound. Then he heard her get their lunch out of the refrigerator and the ding of the microwave.

"Here's some macaroni and cheese, Tito, and some carrot and celery sticks. And your milk, don't forget that."

"I like this stuff," he said, between chomps, his words hard to understand because of all the food in his mouth.

"Finish all of this and I might have some apple slices and a few cookies for you," she said.

Sam walked into the hall and opened the door to the classroom. "Goin' downstairs to the deli for some lunch. You can go when I get back, Jo."

"Not necessary, Sam," she said. "I brought some things from Lorenzo's, you know English food, bland and uninteresting."

"You got that right!" laughed Sam. "Back in thirty."

Once he was downstairs, Sam bought a sandwich and a soda and walked the two blocks to the park that extended along the Willamette River. He sat down on a bench and ate his lunch. Then he punched in the emergency numbers Lorenzo had given him with instructions on when to use them.

Thad Sampson's line went right to voice mail. "This is Thaddeus Sampson, assistant attorney general of Oregon. If you are using this number, it must be an emergency. Leave me contact information and I will return your call as soon as I can."

Sam did as instructed, then placed a second call.

"Greg Nettles, DEA. Who is calling?"

"This is Sam Lincoln. I'm Lorenzo Madrid's law clerk. He said I should call you if an emergency came up."

"Yeah, Sam. I remember you from last year—the lighthouse?'

"Yes, sir, that was me."

"Lorenzo's still gone, I take it."

"Yeah."

"I take it there's some trouble? Okay, don't give me any details. Just sit tight and I'll be there in one hour. You're in Corvallis?"

"Yes, Lorenzo's office."

"The boy? What about the boy?"

"He's okay"

15

LORENZO AND ALBERTO WALKED UP THE HILL looking for the shack Maxine had described. At the top, they reached two houses, one well-kept with a fresh-looking coat of blue paint; the other barely standing, with gaps in the walls and roof and all the windows broken.

"This has got to be the place," said Lorenzo. "I'm going inside."

"We're drawing a crowd, *señor,* said Alberto. "Look."

Lorenzo turned to see at least ten people walking up the hill towards them. "I'm going in," he said. "Distract them while I look around. Tell them I'm official. I look like them so lie a bit. And see if they remember the boy."

"Okay. You're the boss."

Lorenzo turned on the flashlight of his cell phone and moved inside. He could hear Alberto greeting the gathering crowd in a tone of nonchalance.

"*Buenos días. ¿Cómo estás?*" That sort of thing.

He couldn't hear their replies as he moved further into the house. The first room was strewn with overturned furniture and smelled moldy. Two dead rats lay next to a rusty stove. The smell was so bad that Lorenzo took out a handkerchief and held it to his nose. Next was a bedroom, containing a double bed with a

torn and stained mattress and a smaller bed with straw resting on plywood and no mattress. A dresser had no drawers, with a few clothing remnants strewn on the floor beside it. At first glance, the small closet seemed empty but Lorenzo noticed what looked like a deteriorated box sitting on a shelf at the back. As he pulled it down, it slipped out of his hands and fell to the floor in a cloud of dust.

Lorenzo bent over to examine what had fallen out: several pieces of beaded jewelry, a small woven purse, and a baby's blanket. The blanket, in much better condition than anything else in the house, was embroidered with tiny horses. It had been folded around several objects. Lorenzo pulled out an official certificate and several photos inside silver frames.

"BOSS! YOU NEED TO COME OUT!" Alberto's shouts broke his concentration. He stuffed the paper and the photos into the front of his pants and walked quickly outside. The crowd had grown to at least fifty and they looked angry. Alberto had his hands stretched in front of him as if to hold them at bay. As Lorenzo stepped into the sunlight, the people parted to let two policemen walk through their ranks. Both had their guns drawn. Lorenzo walked towards them with his hands up. Alberto ran to his side and began speaking to the policemen in a torrent of Spanish words Lorenzo could barely follow.

The older officer lowered his gun and put it into a holster. The younger, more gung-ho officer, continued to yell at Lorenzo and wave his weapon. He motioned for him to get on the ground. As he started to do so, the older officer put his hand on his colleague's arm and pulled it down.

"*¡Basta!*"

The younger man lowered his gun but kept it in plain sight.

The older officer turned to Alberto. "*Explica, por favor.*"

Alberto turned to Lorenzo. "He's asking us to explain why we are here."

"I got that, Alberto." Then in Spanish he said, "I am a historian doing research on old towns in Ecuador. I apologize for causing a disturbance."

Both officers relaxed. The younger one motioned for the crowd to disperse, and it quickly did just that.

Lorenzo thanked both men for their help. They turned to leave, but the older one asked Alberto under his breath one last question. Alberto shrugged and answered quietly.

The man nodded, smiled, and walked away.

"What did he ask and what did you tell them?"

"He could barely understand your Spanish. I told him you have an L.A. accent."

"Ha, funny, Berto."

They walked down the hill, nodding and smiling to the people who continued to stare at them from the windows and doorways of their houses. When they reached the church, Lorenzo was surprised to find that its doors were locked. He pulled on them repeatedly but they would not budge. "Odd, very odd," he said to Alberto. "He asked us to come back."

At that moment a black Mercedes stopped in front of the church. A uniformed chauffeur got out and opened the rear door. A well-dressed older woman emerged. "We meet again, *Señor* Madrid."

For a moment, Lorenzo did not recognize her or remember how she knew him. "The plane. We talked on the plane." Suddenly, her name registered.

"*Señora Acosta,*" he said, bowing slightly. "What a pleasure to see you again."

Lorenzo walked to meet her, kissing her hand and turning towards a skeptical looking Alberto.

"This is my driver, Alberto. He kindly agreed to be my guide as I try to learn more about your wonderful country."

Alberto stepped in front of Acosta, bowed, and clicked his heels. "*Mucho gusto, señora.*"

"My maid told me about all this commotion," she said. "I was curious so I had my driver bring me here to see what was happening. It isn't often that our humble little town has any visitors except for tourist women looking to buy our Panama hats. And when the visitors are handsome young men like the two of you, all the better."

"Not sure about the 'young' part," said Lorenzo. "Alberto here is the young . . . Have you heard the use of the word *stud?*

"Oh, yes. I raised horses at one time . . ."

"Of course. As I was saying, Alberto is the young stud here."

"You are being too modest," she said.

He turned to Alberto, who looked more than a little embarrassed. "We had probably best drive back to the city now. It's getting late."

"No, no," she said. "I insist that you be my guest for tonight and for dinner. Please humor an old lady and join me. I so seldom have visitors here that it would be a pleasure. I never get to use the English I learned long ago in convent school and I can even get out my best china."

"Alberto? What do you think?"

"You're the boss."

Lorenzo nodded. "Very well. But I have nothing to wear to match your best china."

"Nonsense. I can accommodate that too. My late husband was about your size and his closets are full of fine clothes, including a dinner jacket. I might say that you would look wonderful in a dinner jacket."

Lorenzo glanced at Alberto, who was holding up his hand to hide the big smile on his face.

"What about my colleague here? I can't leave Alberto out of my plans."

"I have plenty of room for the two of you," she said. "In fact, I have a whole wing of the house with many bedrooms that seldom get used. You can even have adjoining rooms if you wish."

Lorenzo blushed at her assumption about the relationship

between him and Alberto. "Alberto is my co-worker, not my lover!"

"Sorry to insult you."

"Oh, it's not an insult," said Lorenzo. "It's just not true in this case."

"All the better," she said, turning toward Alberto. "I will arrange dinner for you and my secretary, Consuelo. She is young and beautiful and very intelligent. Who knows, you might get lucky."

Now it was Alberto's turn to feel his face get red.

16

SAM FOLLOWED NETTLES ADVICE AND "SAT TIGHT" in Lorenzo's office. He could hear Jo and Tito doing lessons in the room next door, so there was no need to disturb their normal morning routine. At ten, he signaled Jo that he was leaving for a few minutes and went downstairs to get coffee and several scones at the Starbucks on the corner, but was gone only ten minutes.

"Who wants to take a break and have a snack?" he said to both of them when he returned.

"WE DO!" they both shouted.

"Tea for you, Jo, and milk for the little man here and coffee for me," he said. "And scones for everyone!"

"What a scone?" asked Tito.

"What *is* a scone, Tito. You need to have a verb in every sentence," said Jo.

"Sorry, Miss Jo. But . . ."

"It's what you've got in your mouth," laughed Sam.

"It's a kind of biscuit," said Jo. "We have eaten them for many years in my country, but now they are popular here."

"Where I come from, we like corn-bread," said Sam. "And you eat a lot of tortillas. I'm sure of that."

"Oh yes, tortillas with honey and sugar," said Tito, as if remembering something pleasant. *"Qué bueno."*

Sam stood up and motioned for Jo to follow him into the office.

"Why not start doing your math, Tito?" she said to the boy, who wiped the remaining crumbs from his mouth and took a last gulp of milk. "I'll be right back."

They stepped through the door and walked far enough away from Tito so he wouldn't hear what they were discussing.

"I called Lorenzo's friend, Greg Nettles. He's the one who rescued us on the coast last year."

"Oh, yes, I remember him. A brave man," said Jo.

"He's coming here soon to talk about how to keep us safe."

"Oh dear," she said, her eyes tearing up. "Not that again."

Sam patted her arm. "I don't know that we're in any danger, but finding the office this way . . ." He looked around and waved an arm as if to encompass the whole room. "It scared me. Lorenzo's instructions were to call both Greg and Thad Sampson. So I did. And Greg said he'd come right over."

"You're doing the right thing, Sam," she said. "Let me know what he says."

"I'll bring you in to hear him yourself. We have no secrets. For better or worse, we're in this thing together."

"Miss Jo," said a voice from the other room. "I'm ready to do a new lesson."

"I'll be right there, Master Tito."

She turned to Sam. "Duty calls."

▫ ▫ ▫ ▫ ▫

Greg Nettles arrived a half hour later. He knocked on the door and spoke in low tones. "Hi Sam. I'm Greg. We met last year during that incident at the Coast."

"Thanks for coming. Sit down. Coffee?"

"Yeah, that would be great."

As Sam set up the coffee maker, Greg walked around the office suite. "Is Lorenzo's office in here?"

"You got it!"

"The classroom's next door?"

"Right again."

He handed Nettles the coffee, who took a sip and drew back. "Wow. Really hot. But I like it to burn my mouth. Keeps me awake."

Nettles motioned toward a closed door. "What's in there?"

"Storage and a small law library."

Nettles nodded towards the door to Lorenzo's office. "Can we talk in there?"

"Sure," said Sam. "There's more room and some privacy in case someone comes in."

"Where's the tutor?" asked Nettles as he sat down in one of the chairs facing Lorenzo's desk. "Jo?"

"Yeah, Jo. She's next door with Tito. We thought it best if we didn't disturb his routine. I want her to hear what you think we should do."

"I'd like to know what I think we should do," he said ruefully. "I owe Lorenzo a lot and I want to help him—and all of you. I just have to figure out how. Tell me exactly what you found when you opened the door this morning."

Sam talked about the condition of the office and how he had put things in order so he wouldn't upset Tito and Jo.

"Maybe I should've waited?" he said, an anguished look on his face. "I guess I screwed up, I mean fingerprints. Right?"

Nettles shook his head. "Don't worry about it. Doubt we would find anything useful. These guys are pros. They don't leave a trace."

"So who are they?" asked Sam. "People hired by that woman who put a hit out on Lorenzo? I mean, forcing his car off the ferry and trying to run him off the road in the mountains."

"Don't think so," said Nettles. "She's long gone and probably as far away from Oregon as possible."

Nettles finished his coffee and set the cup on Lorenzo's desk. "I'm not going to give you all the details, but you need to know a few things about an old case since you're right in the middle of this situation. If my suspicions are correct, they are connected."

Sam leaned forward. "Okay. I'm listening."

"Several years ago, Lorenzo became a key informant in a drug case that started in Salem. No clients were involved. He was in the wrong place at the wrong time, pure and simple. Members of a big Mexican drug gang thought he knew more than he did. He even left the state to teach at the UCLA law school and they followed him there."

"That's where I met him," said Sam. "Right after he finished teaching."

"The end result was that he was kidnapped by these thugs and taken to the desert. He was able to keep in touch with me and we raided the place, rescuing Lorenzo and several other people. In the process, one of our guys shot the big boss. Even though Lorenzo had nothing to do with that, the guys who took over the gang blamed him and have kept trying to find him to kill him ever since."

"No way!" said Sam, shaking his head. "Lorenzo kidnapped and dealing with drug gang bangers? Wow! So they might be the ones who broke in here?"

"I'm thinking that. They may want revenge."

"So what'll we do until Lorenzo gets back?"

"Any idea when that will be?"

"He said he'd be gone a week but it's been ten days already."

"Do you have any way to reach him?"

Sam pulled a piece of paper out of his pocket.

"Kurt Jenkins. Second secretary of the American embassy in Quito, Ecuador," he read and then handed the paper to Nettles.

"Good. I'm going to send Lorenzo a vague message through this guy, to get him back here. I've got my own buddies down there too, I mean DEA buddies. I'll contact them. He needs to get his ass back here."

He turned to Sam. "I'm trusting you even though I don't know you well. If Lorenzo left you in charge of the kid, I know he trusts you a lot. He usually handles things himself, without much help. Here's what we're going to do . . ."

As Nettles made a number of phone calls, Sam briefed Jo and sent her home to pack a bag with clothes for her and the boy. Sam kept Tito with him and had him help put a few books into a bag.

Then Sam called Thad at his office. It only took a brief explanation from him to invite the three of them to stay with him in his house. "Lorenzo is my best friend," he explained. "If he needs my help—if all of you need my help—I'm there for you. I'll see all of you tonight." He gave Sam his address and hung up.

As he ended the conversation, he looked up and saw Tito standing in the doorway to the classroom.

"Are we going to be killed by bad men?" he said through tears.

"Come here, little man."

Sam sat down and Tito walked slowly toward him. Sam hoisted him onto his lap. "Whoa. You are one heavy dude," he said. "We've been feeding you way too much."

Tito snuggled into Sam's chest, tears still running down his cheeks. "Is my papa ever coming back to us, Sam?"

"That he is, that he is."

17

MARGO ACOSTA INSISTED THAT LORENZO RIDE WITH HER. He loved a luxury of a car like a Mercedes. He literally sank into the soft leather seats and hoped the ride would go on forever. Given the life he had chosen, however, buying such a car was not a possibility. His thoughts were interrupted by the beautiful woman sitting beside him. "How do you say it, 'a penny for your thoughts'?"

Lorenzo smiled. I'm sorry. I was just enjoying your wonderful car."

She laughed. "Surely a man of your intellect and good looks could have a career where buying a car like this would be possible. If you want to make a change, I am sure I could arrange many lucrative job opportunities for you."

The car slowed at a tall iron gate. The driver leaned over so he could reach a switch on the intercom, and said, *"Señora Acosta."* The gates swung open and they drove through an archway into a central courtyard. The chauffeur got out and opened the doors, first on Margo's side, then on his. Lorenzo looked back and saw Alberto following closely in his beat up taxi. Lorenzo motioned for him to walk to his side. *"Dios mío. Casa magnifico!"* he said.

The three of them walked into the house as a butler took their bags out of the taxi.

They entered the front hall which

was filled with colonial style Spanish furniture and colorful Indian rugs strewn here and there on the polished tile floor.

"Let's go in here while Edmundo takes your bags to your rooms," she said. "A drink or tea?"

"Too early for me to drink," said Lorenzo. "Tea would be good."

"And you, young man?" she said to Alberto.

He hesitated and glanced at Lorenzo. "Tea also, *por favor, señora.*"

Margo led Lorenzo and Alberto down several steps into an equally grand room with more Spanish furniture, paintings, and various *objets d'art.* One glass case contained what looked like Inca miniatures that belonged in a museum.

Margo pulled on a cord. Within minutes, the butler reappeared carrying a silver tray loaded with a large pot, cups and saucers, and a plate of croissants.

Margo poured the tea and used tongs to place a croissant on each of three napkins. The three drank and ate for a few seconds. Lorenzo noticed that Alberto was eyeing another pastry before Lorenzo had even taken a bite of his. "More croissants?" asked Margo, passing the platter to him. "You are a growing boy, after all."

The three of them laughed as Alberto scooped up three more pastries and ate them quickly, crumbs hanging onto his wispy mustache.

After another half hour of pleasantries, Margo stood up and pulled the cord again. Edmundo appeared instantly. "Please show our young friend to his room. I'll do the same for *Señor* Madrid."

The three stood up and Alberto followed the butler out of the room. She motioned for Lorenzo to sit down.

"We need to talk, Lorenzo. You and I know you are not a tourist. You are a highly respected American attorney. And you are here to defend the American woman who is about to go on trial for kidnapping an innocent Ecuadorian child." She smiled knowingly and waited for his response.

Although taken by surprise, Lorenzo decided it was foolish to lie. Everything she said was true. And just as obvious, Margo had to be the woman who turned Maxine in to the police, probably in this very room. "You know all about me," he said. "Will you have me arrested?"

She laughed and shook her head. "Why would I do such a thing? You have not broken any laws, as far as I know."

Lorenzo smiled too. "No, I have not. I plan to represent my client, Miss March, in your courts where I presume she will get a fair trial. She is innocent of the kidnapping charge. You met her. Did she look like a kidnapper?"

"That is not for me to judge. I am pleased that she has hired a distinguished attorney like you to represent her. Have you ever tried a case in our court system?"

"No, I have not, but I hope to have local counsel to assist me."

"Someone from the embassy no doubt."

"Yes, although I haven't met him yet."

"Why did you come here?"

"I needed to see where the boy lived and where Maxine went when she was here."

"Where is the boy now?"

"In a safe place," said Lorenzo. "And living a better life than he would have lived had he stayed here. I mean, he was an orphan with few prospects."

Her eyes flashed. "Do you mean to tell me that a young boy born in my country has no chance at succeeding in life?"

"I cannot presume to speak for all children in Ecuador, only for the little boy in question."

She stood up and smiled. "No need to quarrel so soon in our relationship."

Lorenzo had not realized that the two of them had a 'relationship,' only a slight acquaintance, but he kept that opinion to himself. He needed this woman and her connections so had to play along with whatever scheme she was concocting.

"Before I take you to your room, let me show you around my house. I am proud of it and its many treasures. I like to share it with good friends like you."

He followed her back into the hall and they walked into a dining room, where the table was set for two, he noticed. A library was next, floor-to-ceiling leather covered books with gold leaf lettering on the bindings filled the shelves.

She stopped at a closed door at the end of the hall. "This is my private sanctuary, my own museum."

They walked into a room containing large display cases filled with what looked like theatrical costumes and props. At the end of the room hung framed prints—movie posters from the 1950s.

"You were a motion picture actress?"

"Alas, I admit it," she said. "Before I got married. My rich snob of a husband did not want me to work, even though I was making more money when I retired than he ever had. I wanted to continue my acting, but he prevailed."

Here was Margo in various roles—as a grand lady, as a prostitute, as a circus clown, as a queen.

"I had no idea, Margo," he said. "Very impressive."

As they walked along the display cases, Lorenzo paused before a set of five posters and a face he was very familiar with. "Is this the American star, Bobbi Bouquet?"

"Oh yes, she was my idol. I even played a minor role in one of her films made in the U.S., I think it was called 'The Bride Wore . . . something or other'."

"*The Bride Wore Blood.*"

"Yes, yes. That was it! How did you know that?"

Lorenzo thought for a moment before answering. He hated to lie, but this was a serious situation. "Bobbi Bouquet is my aunt."

18

SAM WAS ABLE TO GET THE THREE OF THEM OUT OF TOWN in two hours. It helped that he and Jo had already moved into Lorenzo's house. Jo had packed several days worth of Tito's clothes into a duffle bag and then did the same for herself in a suitcase. It had taken Sam just a few minutes to gather up what he would need at Thad's.

Jo and Tito were waiting in the classroom when he got back to the office. "All set?" he asked.

"All set."

"What does 'set' mean?" asked Tito, always the eager student.

"It means we are ready," Jo explained. "Like when you start a foot race, the person standing there says, 'ready, set, go,' and waves a flag and you start running."

"I see."

"I've packed some of his books and games and paper and pencils and pens."

She started to pick up the box, but Sam reached over. "I'll get it," he said. "Unless our strong little man wants to do that!"

He looked down at Tito who stepped forward. He tried to lift the box, but it would not budge. He looked as if he would start to cry.

"Sorry, Tito," said Sam. "I was just kidding. This is almost too heavy even for me. Take this smaller box. That will help me a lot."

The boy smiled and did so. The three of them walked down the stairs to the car. Sam put everything into the trunk, helped Jo get in and then made sure Tito was buckled up snugly in the back seat.

Greg Nettles had been waiting for them to leave. He walked to an unmarked car parked behind their car. He glanced around the area and did not see anyone who wouldn't normally be there. He got in and turned on the ignition.

Sam turned around and shouted, "Who wants to go?"

"We do!" said Jo and Tito.

Both cars pulled out onto Third Street and headed to Highway 99-W for the trip north to Salem.

The dark car with two men inside kept well behind them. When they stopped for lunch at the Burgerville Restaurant in Monmouth, the men pretended to shop at the adjacent convenience store.

Inside the Burgerville, Sam, Jo, Greg, and Tito enjoyed their burgers, fries, and drinks, oblivious to the danger nearby.

19

AS HE WAS PUTTING ON HIS BORROWED DINNER JACKET, Lorenzo realized he had never really dressed for dinner before. He avoided dances in high school because he was never all that interested in girls. Instead, he played the "geek" card to steer them away. He wore glasses and hand-me-down clothes. By the time he was in college, he had come out, at least to himself and close friends. Dances, if any, were all male and never formal. Truth be told, it felt odd to be dancing with another guy in public.

Now here he was looking at himself in the mirror, resplendent in a perfectly cut suit in a mansion in a backwater town in the wilds of a Latin American country where he was a stranger. "On with the show," he muttered, as he walked out into the hall and down the stairs. The ever efficient Edmundo was waiting for him.

"Madame will join you in the drawing room shortly," he said, motioning for Lorenzo to follow him into the room where he and Margo had talked earlier in the day.

"May I offer you a drink, sir?"

"Gin and tonic."

"Right away, sir."

As Edmundo fixed his drink, Lorenzo walked around the room looking at the book titles and authors. All the books were in Spanish and by Latin American or Mexican authors. From Carlos Castaneda to Isabel Allende to Sandra Cisneros, she had them all, plus classics

by Cervantes and Pablo Neruda.

"Here you are, sir. Is there anything else?"

"No thank you, Edmundo."

"Madame will join you soon."

As if on cue, Margo Acosta walked into the room. She was wearing a floor length silk blue gown with a pearl-embroidered bodice, cut just low enough for a tiny bit of cleavage to show. Just the right amount of perfume wafted in the air around her, enough to tantalize, but not to overpower.

"My dear *Señor* Lorenzo," she said, holding out her hand for him to kiss. "You do that dinner jacket justice. My late husband got fat when he grew old so even fine clothes did not improve the way he looked. His boyfriends only liked him for his money and what he could do for them, not his physical attributes."

She was already carrying a martini glass and gestured towards a chair next to a sofa where she sat.

"Dinner will be served shortly. So tell me about yourself."

Lorenzo gave her a brief outline of this life, from growing up in the poverty of East L.A. to college, to setting up a law practice in Oregon.

"And no wife to help you, or kids to raise and be proud of?"

Lorenzo shook his head. "I guess my life is my work."

"*La vida sola,*" she said. "The single life. I envy you in many ways. I have everything I need and more, but I also lead *la vida sola.* I am lonely much of the time, entrapped in my big houses full of art treasures. I could use a man like you at my side."

This conversation was making Lorenzo more and more uncomfortable. In reality, she was his enemy, at least Maxine's. She had caused her arrest and imprisonment. She might even affect Tito's future. Who knew how many right wing connections she had, not only in Ecuador but in the U.S. With the anti-Latino mindset of the current president, anything was possible. He made a quick decision. "What did you have in mind, Margo?"

He moved next to her on the sofa.

"Refresh our drinks, Edmundo, *por favor.*

The butler had reentered the room and quickly made the drinks.

"We will eat in another half hour, Edmundo."

"Yes, madame."

"So tell me about your dear aunt, Bobbi Bouquet. I have admired her for many years, since we appeared together in that movie. She was very kind to a young Latin girl, just out of convent school who knew nothing about the world."

Lorenzo moved closer to Margo on the sofa and turned to face her. "Well, there is not a lot to say other than things you already know. She is my mother's half-sister and they grew apart. They had different fathers. My mother's was Hispanic, hers a rich American banker."

It bothered Lorenzo that these lies came pouring out of him so easily. All for a good cause, he consoled himself. "I saw her only a few times when I was growing up. She would visit my mother and bring clothes and toys to us. Later, I contacted her for money to use for my college tuition."

"So like our darling Bobbi to take care of her own," said Margo.

Although Lorenzo had not known Bobbi long, he doubted she would ever help anyone but herself. "Yes, so true," he said. "A wonderful lady. I owe her a lot."

He needed the fortification of a stronger drink and got up to pour a glass of bourbon. "To continue my story, *señora . . .*"

"Please call me Margo."

"Yes, of course, Margo. We saw one another over the years from time to time. After I had my law degree, I taught at a university in Los Angeles for a time and became acquainted with a movie producer. He hired me to go over actor contracts but wound up asking me to produce a film and the star was . . ."

"Our darling Bobbi."

"The very same, Margo. It was a dream come true for me to

actually work with her professionally." Lorenzo could barely keep from gagging at his outlandish lying.

"I can see why. How grand that it turned out so well."

"Dinner is served, madam." The ever silent Edmundo had reappeared.

Margo stood up and Lorenzo linked her arm with his as they walked into the dining room. The long table was set for two, with Margo at one end and Lorenzo seated to her right. "I thought Alberto and your secretary might be joining us," he said.

"Oh no, they are enjoying each other's company in another part of my house, if you get my meaning," she said, eyes twinkling. "I am sure he is living up to his Latin heritage, I mean by being a perfect gentleman."

She nodded as Edmundo pulled out her chair. Lorenzo sat down in his unassisted, feeling unsteady because of the strong dose of bourbon.

For the next hour, they dined on food that was perfectly prepared. From soup to salad to fish to beef to dessert, everything was excellent. After dinner, the two of them returned to the drawing room.

"A cognac, perhaps?"

"Yes, that would be a nice way to end the evening."

As they sat staring into the fireplace, Margo returned to the subject of Bobbi Bouquet.

"Since you told me about your connection to dear Bobbi, I was thinking how wonderful it would be if I hosted her, I mean at my home in Quito. A film festival, perhaps."

"I am sure she would love it," he said. "And it would be wonderful for her to reconnect with old friends like you."

"Do you really think so? I mean I was practically an extra. I spoke only a few lines, as I recall."

"Believe me, Bobbi would remember you, especially if you are asking her to be in a festival of her pictures."

"I hope so. Do you think there is a chance?"

"More than a chance," he said. "It will happen!"

Lorenzo glanced at the large clock on the mantle. "It is late. I should let you go to bed and I need rest too. We will be driving to Quito tomorrow and then flying back to the U.S. the day after."

"So soon," said Margo, a sad look on her face. "You must visit me again and stay longer."

"You are a gracious lady and I will. When I return, I will have news of Bobbi and her interest in the film festival."

"Oh, I hope so. It would be my dearest wish to see her again and talk about the, how do you say it, good old days."

As he bowed to kiss Margo's hand again, she suddenly grabbed him and kissed him on the mouth. He pretended to enjoy the kiss. "So good to spend time with you, Margo," he said. "Thank you for your hospitality."

As they parted, Lorenzo thought that he was not the only one in the room who stretched the truth to the breaking point.

20

LORENZO GOT UP VERY EARLY THE NEXT MORNING, wanting to get away before he got talked into having a long breakfast with Margo or being invited into her bedroom. He knocked softly on Alberto's door. No response. He knocked more forcefully. Still no response. So he tried the door which was unlocked. He opened it slowly.

In the dim light, Lorenzo could see Alberto asleep in a big four poster bed near the window. Stepping closer to pull on his foot, he could see that his compatriot was not alone. His arms were wrapped around the naked body of Margo's secretary.

He cleared his throat. Still nothing. He bent down next to Alberto's ear. "¡DESPIERTA! GET UP!"

Alberto sat up immediately, looking embarrassed. "Oh boss. I am sorry. I have failed you."

By this time, the young woman had stirred and was pulling the covers over her body. Unlike Alberto, she didn't seem all that perturbed.

"Just get up and pack fast. We've got to get on the road!" said Lorenzo.

As he walked out of the room, he heard the woman say, "Oh baby. Don't leave me," or something to that effect. The thought crossed his mind that this incident had nothing to do with Alberto, his looks, or his sexual prowess. Sleeping with Margo's houseguests was very much part of her job description. He was

grateful that he had escaped a similar fate.

Back in his room, Lorenzo wrote a note of thanks to Margo, promising to return in a few weeks with Bobbi Bouquet.

Alberto met him in the front hall, yawning and rubbing his eyes. The ever present Edmundo was standing by the open door.

"Please give this note to madame. I have to be on my way and did not want to disturb her."

"Very well, *Señor* Madrid. I hope we will be seeing you again. I could tell that madame likes your company."

"And thank you for taking such good care of us," said Lorenzo as he got into the passenger seat of the beat up taxi.

Edmundo seemed to be repelled by the look of the old jalopy. "I could order the car to take you back to Quito. I am sure madam would not mind."

"No, thank you. We will see you again soon."

At that point, Alberto gunned the engine, which backfired and belched several puffs of black smoke before lurching forward down the driveway. The gates opened at a stately pace and, for a moment, Lorenzo thought they would crash through them.

After several miles of silence, Alberto turned to Lorenzo with a pained look on his face. "*Dios mío*, Lorenzo. I am ashamed that you will no longer think of me as a professional."

"No, don't worry. You are a young man and hormones are hormones. The *señorita* is very beautiful."

"Did you do such things when you were a youth?"

Too complicated and "un-macho" to tell the truth, thought Lorenzo. "Not exactly," he said. "Just remember in situations like that the women who come after you may not have your best interests at heart. She was on a mission from her boss, Margo Acosta, to find out why we are here."

"She didn't ask me about stuff like that," he said. "We just drank some wine and played around and then started having sex. Really good sex, *señor.*"

"Glad to hear it," said Lorenzo, turning his head to hide the smile on his face.

"One thing I don't get, boss."

"What's that?"

"This *Señora* Acosta is the one who turned in your friend and really caused this whole problem for you and the little boy and Maxine."

"Yes, you're right."

"Why would you trust her? Why would you think she would help you and your friend?"

Lorenzo smiled. "There are so many details I didn't know. My friend was upset when she was here and has been through a lot since then. I don't trust her recollections of what happened. I thought I'd get it from what we call 'the other side.'"

"Your enemies?"

"Right, my enemies. In the legal profession—or life in general—it is best to keep your friends close and your enemies closer."

Alberto thought for a moment. "Hey, boss. I like that saying. I learn from you every time I am with you. I like that."

Lorenzo leaned back in the seat. "I'm going to take a nap for a few minutes."

Alberto drove on, a smile on his face, thinking, "Friends and enemies. Keep the latter closer than the former. I'll remember that."

21

A HALF HOUR LATER, ALBERTO TOUCHED LORENZO ON THE ARM. "Boss. Someone is following us."

Lorenzo shook his head as if to shake off the cobwebs of sleep. "What?"

"Some guys in a pickup truck. They are hanging back as we go through these small towns but I don't like the way it looks. When we get back out into the countryside, they might try to force us off the road or something bad like that."

Lorenzo turned around. He couldn't make out faces or even tell how many there were in the truck.

"There are guys in the back of the truck too," said Alberto, a worried look on his face. "I don't like it. I don't have a gun. I would not have any way to protect you if they tried something."

"Why would anyone be after me? No one knows anything about me."

"Except *Señora Acosta*," he said. "She is bad news for you and me both."

Lorenzo pulled his cell phone out of a pocket and punched in the number of Kurt Jenkins at the embassy. *"No servicio,"* he read from the screen. "Shit," he muttered.

"You can say that again many times over," said Alberto, pushing his foot on the accelerator. "This jalopy has no power."

At that point, steam started pouring out of the radiator. The brakes barely worked, but Alberto steered the car off the road onto a dirt side road. Even though by then the engine had stopped running, the car kept moving down a hill. He stopped it by deliberately ramming it into some heavy brush. By this time, the pickup had almost reached them.

"Run boss, run!" shouted Alberto as he pushed the door open and held it as a shield against the bullets that ricocheted off it and the ground around him.

Lorenzo rushed out and plunged into the heavy brush, its thorny leaves scratching his arms and face. He looked back towards Alberto, who stood up and started to run toward the bushes himself. As he did so, a bullet hit him and he fell to the ground. "I'm hit, boss! Keep running!"

This can't be happening, Lorenzo muttered to himself. It's not worth a man's life. Maxine will have to get out of prison on her own. Tito is the one I have to help, not her. If I get out of this alive, that's what I'll concentrate on.

Even through the thick underbrush, he could get a clear look at the men. They were dressed in fatigues. By the agility of their movements, they seemed young. He couldn't see their faces, however, because their heads were covered by the balaclavas worn by terrorists everywhere.

"*Mira! Mira! El hombre está aquí!*" said a voice behind him.

Lorenzo had been concentrating on the two men walking toward him and hadn't noticed that there was a third. The three formed a circle around Lorenzo and then one pulled him to his feet.

"*Muy bonito,*" said the guy who had come from behind. He put his gun under Lorenzo's chin and used it to push his head up. He found this funny so kept doing it. Then he ran his hands up and down Lorenzo's body as if looking for weapons. When he got to his testicles, he squeezed them tightly. When Lorenzo winced in pain, he laughed again.

"*¡Basta!*" said the apparent leader. He pushed the gun away and gave the younger man a shove. *"Estupido! Muy estupido!"*

The other man stepped behind Lorenzo and tied his hands.

"Americano! Americano!" said Lorenzo loudly, hoping his identity would let them know he was not your run-of-the-mill Ecuadorian peasant. *"Muy importante! Muy importante!"*

The leader only laughed and pointed back towards the truck.

As Lorenzo walked past Alberto's body he tried to stop to at least check his pulse. The hotheaded one tried to pull him back, but Lorenzo ignored him and took off his jacket to drape it over the body. This time, the thug hit Lorenzo in the stomach so forcefully that he doubled over in pain. He fell on his side opposite Alberto's face. As Lorenzo glanced at his dead friend, Alberto's eyes opened and he winked at Lorenzo.

22

THE MOVE TO SALEM WENT SMOOTHLY. Thad was waiting for them at his house in the south part of Salem. Greg pushed by him and quickly checked all the rooms in the house, trying windows and outside doors.

"Welcome to you all," Thad said, as he helped Sam carry in their bags and the boxes of Tito's books and school paraphernalia.

"Gotta run," said Greg as he hurried out the door. "I'll be in touch."

"That's Greg," said Sam. "What are your neighbors going to think of this invasion of brown and black people. This is a pretty fancy area."

"Did you have a good look at my skin color?" said Thad. "They're used to me. Besides, this is the state capitol, not some backwater town with lots of rednecks."

"What's a redneck?" said a tiny voice from the small person standing next to Jo. The three looked at one another and at Tito. "It's when someone doesn't like people who don't have white skin," said Thad.

"But you don't need to worry, dar-lin'," said Jo. "Everyone likes Tito."

"How could they not?" added Sam.

"The three of you settle in and I'll see you about six," said Thad. "I need to get back to work."

"Will you allow me to cook dinner?" asked Jo.

"That would be great," said Thad. "I tend to eat take-out meals every night. However, I stocked up on food, so check out what I have in the refrigerator and call me if you need anything else."

The three of them spent the rest of the day getting acquainted with the house and starting their new routines. After Jo and Tito were working on math and reading, Sam called Greg.

"Glad you called, Sam. You guys doing okay? Any strange people walking or driving by who look like they don't belong there?"

"No one," said Sam. "Things couldn't be better. Lorenzo's got a lot of good friends."

"I sent him a message through the embassy in Ecuador asking him to contact me. "I haven't heard anything yet. It takes a while. I'm going to insist that he return home immediately."

"Sounds good to me, Greg."

"Call me if anything strange happens. I mean like a car out of place, a person who seems to be watching the house. Anything like that. Those people in Corvallis shouldn't be able to find you."

"I'm not worried, Greg. But I'll feel a whole lot better when Lorenzo gets back. I'm only 24 years old. This is a pretty heavy burden for me."

"I hear ya, kid. It'll be over soon."

23

ONE OF THE BLACK-HOODED GUYS YANKED LORENZO TO HIS FEET and shoved him toward the truck. "You are much too pretty to kill yet," said the man. "We need to have some fun with you!"

"Your English is pretty good, for an Ecuadorian peasant," said Lorenzo, spitting blood.

Lorenzo braced for another blow but the man held back.

"We do not want damaged goods," he said, pulling up Lorenzo's head so they could all see his face.

"¡*Maricón!*" he shouted. The others soon joined in.

"¡*Maricón!* ¡*Maricón!*"

Was he that obvious? Lorenzo never thought of himself as acting effeminate. Young men did hit on him—or try to—all the time. But he never invited such attention. He guessed this reaction stemmed from misplaced Latin *machismo* more than anything else. But how could he be contemplating his masculinity at a time like this? He shook his head. Maybe the blow to the stomach had upset his equilibrium.

The man pushed him into a circle that the other men had formed. This was to be a true "gang bang," he thought, remembering a slang phrase used by the tough guys in his L.A. neighborhood.

He began to stagger and contort his face into something grotesque, like he did when he played the Quasimodo in a

production of "The Hunchback of Notre Dame" in college. Then he started limping and moaning and actually drooling.

"I like you," he said to the shortest man in the gang. By his short stature, dark skin, and straight black hair, Lorenzo guessed he was probably an Indian. The leader and several others had the light skin, fine features and good looks of those of Spanish heritage. *"Tu maricón tambien?"*

The man looked horrified and pulled away as Lorenzo attempted to kiss him. The others started laughing at both of them. Lorenzo turned back to the *macho* leader and stepped forward to continue his charade. *"¡BASTA!* Get away from me!" the man shouted, pushing Lorenzo away.

Suddenly a shot rang out and Lorenzo saw a hole appear in the middle of the man's balaclava right between his eyes. The man tried to raise his hand, but collapsed before he could touch his face. The others panicked and began to run in all directions. Several of them were shot too, but in their legs and arms.

Lorenzo had run into the brush as soon as his captor had been shot. He peered out cautiously to see about ten men dressed in Army camouflage enter the clearing from all sides. He walked out with his hands up. "I'm an American! I'm an American!"

"As Stanley said to Livingston," said one of the men, 'Mr. Lorenzo Madrid, I presume.'" Both men grinned.

"Staff Sergeant James Porten, Mr. Madrid, U.S. Army Special Forces. The embassy sent us out to find you."

"Whew! To say I'm relieved is putting it mildly!"

"What about me?" said a voice from behind.

Lorenzo turned to see two of the soldiers supporting Alberto. "God, Alberto, I forgot about you! I'm sorry! Are you okay?"

"Just a flesh wound," said one of the men, who had a red cross on one sleeve.

"I didn't worry as much after you winked at me back there."

"I played dead, and for a while, I thought I was dead."

"Alberto Dragón is a good friend of mine. This is Sergeant

Porten." The two shook hands.

"I've seen you around the embassy," said Alberto.

"I've seen you, too," said Porten. "Let's get you patched up. We've got a setup a few hundred yards that way. Food and hot coffee and a radio."

"That's the best news I've heard in days," said Lorenzo.

◻ ◻ ◻ ◻ ◻

At the camp, the medic bandaged Alberto's wound as Porten led Lorenzo into the back of the van. Another soldier was sitting in front of a bank of monitors. "Get the embassy on the line, sergeant."

"Yes sir." He began to move the dials in front of him, soon the static cleared, and a voice said, "Special Operations." The sergeant gave him several numbers, presumably to authenticate he was authorized to make the call. "Who do you want to talk to, sir," the sergeant said, turning to Lorenzo.

"Second Secretary Kurt Jenkins."

The sergeant repeated the name.

"Kurt Jenkins."

The sergeant motioned Lorenzo to sit in his seat. "Mr. Jenkins. This is Lorenzo Madrid."

"God, Lorenzo, it's good to hear from you! Are you okay?"

"Yeah, more or less."

"And Alberto? Is he okay too."

"Yeah, but maybe a little banged up. Sergeant Porten and his men saved us from God knows what gang had captured us."

"I sent Porten out to look for you. You didn't check in like you said you would."

"Sorry, I guess I didn't. I get so used to doing things on my own, I ignore offers of help. It's a failing of mine."

"A failure that could have gotten you and Alberto killed! You're in a foreign country and you don't know the rules of survival!"

"Sorry, I won't let it happen again."

"Did you find out anything useful?"

"A great deal. I'll fill you in when I get back to the embassy."

"Good. Let me talk to Porten."

Lorenzo moved out of the seat and the sergeant slid in. He thought it best to go back outside. "Thanks for your help," he said to the communications man.

"No problem, sir."

Lorenzo walked over to a small tent with a red cross on the flap. Alberto was sitting on a cot, his shirt off and the medic placing a large gauze pad on his shoulder. His head already had a bandage wrapped around it. "Hi, Alberto. How are you doing?"

"I've been better, I guess." His eyes were now bloodshot and he looked exhausted.

"He'll be fine," said the medic. "Just a flesh wound on his head and a scrape on his shoulder."

"I'm right outside, Alberto," said Lorenzo. "I'm not leaving until you're able to go with me."

"Sounds good, *señor.*"

Lorenzo walked over to Porten who had just emerged from the communications van. "So what's the plan, sergeant?"

"You are to be extracted late today."

"What does that mean?"

"It means that a small helicopter will land in a helipad clearing we set up a half mile or so away, and you'll get on the bird and fly away."

"A helicopter? That is a surprise. I figured we'd drive back to Quito the same way we got here."

"Second secretary Jenkins thinks that would be too dangerous. You are high profile now because of your defense of Ms. March. Our government does not want any more incidents before her trial. Trust me, this is a better way to get you guys out of here, fast and safe."

"Do we know who those guys were?" asked Lorenzo. "And how did they know I was even here? Although come to think of it, the secretary told me he has intelligence that points to a renegade group from MS-13. Man, they're creepy and scary looking with all the tattoos."

"You were well-informed, sir," said Porten. "That's them. MS-13 is short for *Mara Salvatrucha.* That translates to 'Salvadoran street posse.' We think there are as many as 10,000 of them. They are young guys who grew up in the U.S., mainly L.A. Many of them were sent back to El Salvador, where they were from originally. Once there, they set up a real criminal enterprise involving drugs and people trafficking. They have pretty much taken over the government of El Salvador. The police and even the army have no control over them. Recently, they have started spreading their terror southward. The ambassador thinks the guys who attacked you were from MS-13. They are ruthless. I have no doubt that they would have killed Alberto and tortured you before trying to get the government to pay ransom for your return."

"Why me? How do they even know about me?"

"Not sure. We will know more when we interrogate the three we captured with you. They are small links in the chain but one of them might talk in exchange for leniency. These guys usually join gangs for money to feed their families or for drugs to sell or to use themselves."

"God," said Lorenzo. "This is all I need."

"Maybe it's because of your defense of Ms. March," said Porten. He thought for a moment. "Have you ever encountered drug gangs in the U.S., I mean as a defense or prosecuting attorney?"

He had indeed had a continuing problem with a particular gang in Oregon, but it was too farfetched to have any connection to this. "Nothing that would be relevant," he said.

Porten looked up as another one of his men approached carrying two trays of food. "Thanks sergeant."

He turned to Lorenzo. "The food's not too bad. The powers that be know what we go through out here so they try to send the real stuff—meat, vegetables, cereal, noodles, milk, butter, eggs. Stuff like that. And beer."

He uncapped a bottle of Budweiser and handed it to Lorenzo, who gulped it down quickly.

"Have another, sir," he said, handing a second beer to Lorenzo who drank half of it.

"I guess I needed the fortification," he laughed. "I don't usually drink very much."

Whatever it takes, sir," said Porten. "You've been through a very bad experience. I'm amazed that you're handling it as well as you are."

The food—spaghetti, meatballs, garlic bread, and a salad—was very good and even hot. Lorenzo ate it fast. "Really great food, sergeant. My compliments to the chef."

"HASTINGS! Get yourself out here!"

A young specialist walked out from the mess tent, a worried look on his face. He looked like he belonged in junior high not in the jungles of South America. "Sir? Is something wrong?"

"Our guest here, Mr. Madrid, thinks your food is great. No matter how much I try to talk him out of saying that, he keeps repeating himself."

The specialist smiled. "Thank you, SIR!"

The two of them sat for a while, finishing their beers. "I'd like to ask you a few questions, if I could, staff sergeant."

"Fire away, sir. I'll answer them if I can."

"You seem familiar with the March situation."

"I am that, yes, sir. I was on that mission."

"I had no idea. What can you tell me about that raid that almost freed her?"

Porten lowered his voice. "I was acting as a medic because we were shorthanded. I'm usually in counterterrorism but was an EMT at home so I got recruited into the rescue mission. It failed miserably. Two of our men were shot, including our commander, Curtis DeStefano. He was from Special Forces but had been detailed to the State Department for embassy security in hot areas like here."

"I'm sorry for your loss. Was someone else there too, I mean someone not normally in your squad?"

"I guess you know about Colonel Bickford."

Lorenzo didn't know many of the details but he pretended he did. "I know he and your squad tried to rescue Maxine March from that prison. I had heard some of your group were killed and badly wounded."

"Yes, as I said, two dead and five wounded. Someone had tipped off the guards in the prison that we were coming. We stormed that gate and a whole line of them were there, rifles drawn. We didn't have a chance."

"How'd you get away?"

"We ran like hell, dragging the dead and wounded with us. The soldiers were reloading. Maybe they had old rifles, I'm not sure, but they had to stop to reload. That saved us." Porten was tearing up at the memory.

"Sorry to make you relive this, Porten. One last question: Was the colonel one of the dead you pulled out?"

"Oh, no, sir, he was alive when we pulled him out—badly wounded, but alive. But by the next morning, he had disappeared. We found only bloody clothing and discarded bandages on his cot."

At that moment, they heard the whirring sound of helicopter rotors and soon after, two small aircraft landed in the nearby clearing. "We go now, sir!" shouted Porten. He signaled for Alberto to be brought forward and the three of them ducked their heads as they neared the first helicopter. A crewman helped them step up and pointed to seats on each side of the aircraft. They sat down and buckled up.

"YOU GOING TOO?" shouted Lorenzo.

Porten nodded. "NO SCREWUPS THIS TIME. YOU'RE A PRECIOUS CARGO!"

Almost immediately, the helicopter took off. As they did so, Lorenzo saw the three gang members being shoved into the second aircraft.

▫ ▫ ▫ ▫ ▫

The flight to Quito took about a half hour and they landed, once again, in an official section of the airport. A car with diplomatic license plates was waiting for them and the three of them got in quickly and it sped off.

"Mr. Jenkins has had your belongings moved from the hotel to the embassy," said Porten. "You'll be staying there until you leave Ecuador. I guess that's just a few days from now?"

"That's the plan. But why am I being moved?"

"You need to ask Mr. Jenkins that question."

"I can only guess but maybe I have become too high profile, given the publicity surrounding the hearing for Maxine March."

"I don't know, sir. I can't say."

They drove in silence for a half hour and then slowed down at the entrance to the American embassy. The gates slowly opened and the car sped through. Lorenzo turned around. "Were we being followed?"

"Maybe, but I'm not sure," said Porten. "We're not taking any chances with you after what happened out there." He turned to look at Alberto. "You too. You're to check into the medical clinic and then, when you're well, you'll get a room here too. No chance to go home. We'll get you some clothes."

"Wow. I've never stayed in the embassy before. Pretty cool."

Porten smiled. We don't want you to be picked up and held for ransom or anything like that."

"Because you know, Alberto," Lorenzo said with a straight face, "we might decide not to pay it!"

Alberto had a horrified look on his face, until Lorenzo and Porten started laughing. "Misplaced Yankee humor," said Alberto, shaking his head in disgust.

The car stopped at a four story building well inside the grounds of the embassy. They got out and a Marine guard opened the door for them.

"Welcome, Mr. Madrid," said a pretty girl who got up from a desk. "I'm the concierge here at the guest house. She handed two card keys to Lorenzo, one for him and the other, presumably, for Alberto. "You are upstairs on the third floor." She pointed to a map of the building. "And you are here," she said to Alberto, handing him a map. You'll be with our live-in staff on this floor. But first, you're expected in the medical unit. I'll ask the guard to escort you there."

"Thanks very much for your help . . ." Lorenzo looked at her name tag, "Miss Szabo."

"Please let me know if I can help you with anything during your stay with us."

"I will do that."

Porten took his arm and directed him to the elevator.

"You're going with me?" asked Lorenzo.

"I want to check out the room for myself, to see if everything looks okay."

"Okay, thanks. But I think I can take care of myself from here on out."

"Humor me, sir. In my business, you learn early on never to take any chances."

"You're the boss, sergeant."

They arrived at the room in a few seconds and Porten put his arm out to stop Lorenzo from going in. He used a card to open the door. He walked in slowly with his hand on a gun tucked into his waistband. "All clear, sir. You can come in."

Lorenzo walked into a pleasant, though sparingly furnished room with two beds, a dresser, a leather sofa and matching recliner, a table and four chairs, and two floor lamps.

"Home sweet home, sir," smiled Porten.

"This will do nicely, sergeant. Thanks for everything. Will you go back to the jungle now?"

"I'll take a few days leave here in Quito and then go out there. But not for too long. My deployment here is almost over."

"Where to after here?"

"If I told you, I'd have to kill you," laughed Porten.

After Porten left, Lorenzo opened his briefcase and stacked his files on the table. He needed to work on his approach for Maxine's hearing scheduled for the day after tomorrow. And then he could go home.

24

MUCH TO LORENZO'S SURPRISE, Jenkins insisted that they take an embassy car to the court building. Lorenzo had sent his best suit and shirt to the embassy laundry so he looked professional.

"As I've said, this case has generated a lot of publicity in the media here in Ecuador," Jenkins explained, as they got into the car. "The ambassador and I decided that we might as well show the flag a bit and come out publicly in our support of Ms. March and the boy. We can't have another incident like Lori Berenson where Maxine is tried under questionable circumstances and locked away in a remote prison in the Andes where she could die. Shining a light on this whole thing is the best course to take."

"That will make it easier for me, at least I hope it will," said Lorenzo. "I don't know the courts here at all. This will be heard in the Supreme Court, so we're dealing with judges, not juries who might be swayed by the boy and the woman trying to save him. It all depends on the judge or judges."

"I gather there might be several of them to decide the case, but only one today," said Jenkins. "That's the way their judicial system works. You'll have the help of our legal attaché, when the actual trial begins. He's on home leave right now."

"What about Maxine March? Is she here?"

"Yes, she was brought down from the prison yesterday."

"I need to talk to her before we go in."

"I've set that up, but for only a half hour or so and in the holding cell with her behind bars."

"Not ideal, but I suppose it will have to do,"

At that moment, they drove up to the court building. As they got out to walk up the long expanse of steps, a group of reporters noticed them and came running. The taunts and questions came fast, some in English, some in Spanish.

"Are you the lawyer who is representing the kidnapper?"

"You are very handsome. Are you and *Señorita* March sleeping together?"

"What right have you to come to our courts to save someone like this kidnapper?"

"Justice for the *niño!* When do we see him? Are you hiding his abuse?"

"Are you a kidnapper too?"

The group followed Lorenzo and Jenkins and the security guard/chauffeur up the steps, surrounding them and jostling them until they reached the main entrance. There, two uniformed guards pushed them behind the barricades on either side. The shouts continued. Just as Lorenzo started to walk through the doors, he turned and shouted, *"¡BASTA! SEÑORA* MARCH *ES INOCENTE!"*

That remark brought boos and eye rolls and more shouts from the crowd. They continued to chant, *"SECUESTRADORA! SECUESTRADORA!"* "KIDNAPPER! KIDNAPPER!"

The doors closed and they walked across the wide lobby to the security checkpoint. Jenkins flashed his diplomatic credentials and a temporary one for Lorenzo and the guard waved them through.

An older man dressed in a well-cut suit stepped forward. Lorenzo's eyes immediately focused on his large handlebar mustache.

"Señores. Sebastión Blanco. Bienvenido. I am the senior

administrator of the Supreme Court of the sovereign nation of Ecuador. I am at your service. I will take you to your client and then to the courtroom. Please follow me."

The two of them shook hands with Blanco and then followed him across the lobby and down a long hallway, its tile-covered floor sparkling in the light from the crystal chandeliers. The walls were covered with beautiful murals and mosaic scenes.

Halfway down, Blanco stopped and opened a small door next to the grand carved doors Lorenzo figured led to the courtroom. He motioned for them to enter. Halfway across the small room, bars blocked the way. Inside what was essentially a cage, Maxine March stood to greet them.

"*Diez minutos,*" said Blanco as he walked out the door.

The minute she saw them, Maxine cried, "My God it is so good to see you both! You can't know how much I value this break from the prison. And also to know that the two of you are on my side. I've felt pretty hopeless since I was arrested." She held her hand to her mouth, but could not smother a violent coughing fit. "Excuse me," she said when it finally subsided.

"We are very glad to see you, too, Ms. March," said Lorenzo adopting a formal tone, handing her a handkerchief. He put a finger to his lips and pointed to the light fixture. He was quite sure that somewhere in the room, their words were being taped. He pulled out a notepad.

Talk in generalities. I'm sure we're being taped.
This is a preliminary hearing to see if they will
bind you over for trial. I'm sure they will.

"So how are things at home? I hope everyone is well."

Lorenzo gave her a thumbs up. "Here is what will happen today. We will walk into the courtroom and face the judge. I'll be standing beside you, and I have asked them to remove your shackles. Stand up straight and try not to cry. You are not to speak at all. I will do the talking. The judge will read the charges and you will then plead. This is the only time you will speak. Say *'inocente'* in a loud and clear voice, and that will be it for today. Then you will go back to the prison and I go home and get to work. Not sure how long it will take to get your day in court." He turned to Jenkins.

"This is a high profile case that the government may want to get out of the way," Jenkins said. "Maybe a month."

Maxine's shoulders slumped as Lorenzo scribbled out another note on the pad.

Tito is thriving. Good in school and a good boy always. He has people around him who care about him.

Does he ask about me? (Maxine wrote.)

Everyday. Where is mama? When is she coming back to me?

The truth was, Tito never asked about her anymore. Lorenzo brought up her name from time to time, but that was met with a shrug of his little shoulders. Lorenzo knew that would change when she returned. If she returned! Lorenzo fought the thought that he hoped that day would never come. He loved that little boy more than anyone in his life. But if she got out of this mess, she would certainly deserve to have him back in her life. If that happened, he could only hope they settled nearby so he could see Tito often. Time would determine that.

Blanco opened the door to signal that their time with Maxine was up.

"We'll see you next door in a few minutes," said Jenkins. "Keep up your faith. Lorenzo is really good at what he does."

"I know, I know," she sobbed, as the guard returned and signaled her to sit down on the cot by the back wall of the cell.

Lorenzo and Jenkins followed Blanco into the hallway. "You know, Kurt," he said, "I appreciate your confidence in me but I'm beginning to think it will take a miracle to work all of this out."

As they headed to the courtroom, the crowd of media people who had accosted them outside was rushing down the hall towards them. *"SECUESTRADORA! SECUESTRADORA!* KIDNAPPER! KIDNAPPER!"

25

EVERYTHING WAS GOING WELL IN OREGON. Jo and Tito continued their studies together in the makeshift classroom they'd set up in Thad's study. Sam kept up with Lorenzo's case load, filing continuances when necessary and doing research on cases that had not yet gone to trial. In the evenings after Thad came home and the four of them had dinner, Sam drove to the law library at Willamette University across town.

Tito took to Thad right away, largely because he acted very much like Lorenzo, a gentle soul who was smart and good at what he did. Thad started playing with Tito in the evenings. That gave Jo a break and the chance to get away from her duties. She usually drove into town with Sam and had dinner at a nice tearoom near the Salem Public Library.

Thad was teaching Tito how to play dominos one night, when the boy walked over to him and started crying. Thad let him crawl onto his lap. "What's wrong, *Señor* Tito? Why are you crying?

"My papa has left me," he said between sobs. "I think I made him mad. I always try to be a good boy but I was not good enough, I guess."

By this time, his little body was shaking. Thad pulled him close. "Oh no, Tito, you are wrong. Your papa loves you very much. He told me so before he left on this trip."

"Really? Are you sure?"

"Yes, my good man, I am very sure.

He will be back to us soon and you will see that I am right."

"Really?" More sniffles.

"Really. Would I lie to you? We are good friends, right?"

"Yes, I guess," he said, blowing his nose and dabbing at his eyes with the handkerchief Thad gave him.

"You GUESS! We are *amigos* forever! Let's have some ice cream before I put you to bed. Okay?"

The two of them walked into the kitchen where Thad lifted the boy onto a stool and filled a small bowl with chocolate fudge ice cream. They bantered back and forth for a few more minutes and then Thad lifted the boy down. "Put your pajamas on and brush your teeth and I'll be in to tuck you in."

"What does 'tuck' mean?"

"It means I will make sure you are covered up with blankets so you will keep warm all night. And I'll push them under the mattress so you won't throw them off and get cold."

"Okay, I understand."

Ten minutes later Thad stopped at the door and turned back to Tito. "Lights on or off?"

"On, *por favor.*"

Thad sat down with a sigh in the living room, but soon the buzzing of his cell phone broke the blissful silence. "Thad Sampson."

"Mr. Sampson, it's Jo, Tito's teacher," she said with a catch in her voice.

"What's wrong?"

"It's Sam. He wasn't at the law library when I went to meet him. I went inside and no one had seen him. It's not like him to do that. He is very dependable. God help us all if something has happened to him! I remembered where he usually studies so I went there. His books were on the table and his favorite thermos cup had been tipped over, the coffee spilled all over the table. God help us all!"

❖❖❖❖❖

26

COURT GUARDS KEPT THE MEDIA MOB FROM FOLLOWING LORENZO into the courtroom. *"NO ENTRADA! NO ENTRADA!"* they shouted, physically picking up a short TV cameraman and setting him down away from the door. He retreated with a stunned look on his face. The reporter with him, a beautiful woman with long flowing hair, protested loudly but moved away from the doors too. As she did so, she winked at Lorenzo as he passed. Her tight dress and high heels diverted the attention of some of the other reporters so the guards could close the doors as they gaped at her shapely body.

Blanco, the court administrator, met them and led them down the long aisle to a wooden barrier. He opened a gate and they walked to one of two tables facing the judge's bench. Lorenzo sat down and looked around the ornate chamber. It was beautiful with a cathedral-like ceiling of mosaic murals depicting, he supposed, scenes of Ecuadorian history. Carved wooden beams extended from the ceiling to the tile floor.

A middle-aged woman was already sitting at the table. She extended her hand to both Lorenzo and Jenkins. "Laura Nieto, your translator."

"The embassy is paying her for now," whispered Jenkins. "We'll settle up on this later. You can trust her."

Blanco leaned over and whispered to them. "His Excellency Jorge Ponte is

handling this case."

A side door opened and two guards led Maxine into the chamber. She looked terrible. Her face looked even paler than it had less than an hour before in the holding cell. Worse, both arms were shackled. Lorenzo started to get up to protest, but Blanco shook his head, so he sat back down. At that moment a side door opened and the judge walked in. They all stood.

The judge looked like he was out of central casting—a tall and slim, middle-aged man with a carefully trimmed goatee and pencil thin moustache. He was wearing a black robe with gold trim on the sleeves and at the collar.

In swiftly spoken Spanish, Blanco announced the convening of the court and recited the judge's name and rank. Lorenzo didn't catch everything that was said, but got the part about Ponte being a senior judge. He put on tiny wire-rimmed glasses and motioned for them all to sit.

"I am convening this hearing to determine if the defendant . . ." He looked at a sheet of paper in front of him . . . "*Señorita* Maxine March, should be held over for trial for the crime of kidnapping."

Lorenzo jumped to his feet. "May I speak, your excellency?"

The judge held up his hand. "I am not finished, Mr. . . ." he looked at the paper . . . "Madrid. Like the capitol of Spain, the home of my ancestors." He looked at Lorenzo. "Your's too?"

"Yes, your excellency." Lorenzo sat down.

In Spanish, Ponte read from a two page summary of the case, with Laura whispering the translation to Lorenzo to be sure he understood. The judge took off his glasses and looked at Lorenzo. "Now, you may speak, *Señor* Madrid."

"*Gracias, su excelencia.* What I wanted to say was that the charge of kidnapping has not yet been proven. I understood that was the purpose of this hearing. My client, *Señorita* March, has not yet been formally charged for anything. She has been held against her will for . . ."

"*Sí, sí, sí.* I know all of these things. Even with all the evidence against her, I suppose we must presume her innocence at this point."

Lorenzo looked at Maxine who had slumped in her chair. "Take it easy, Lorenzo," whispered Jenkins. "It won't help anyone if you pick a fight with the judge."

"*Gracias, su excelencia.* We appreciate your understanding."

What followed was the testimony of a series of people who Maxine had encountered when she arrived in Ecuador: her interview at the immigration ministry where she claimed to be looking into adopting a child for friends in the U.S.; her trip to Montecristi where the desk clerk at the hotel described her travels around the town; and the local policeman who found her in the ruined house of Tito's family. They were all paraded before the judge and left the courtroom after they had testified.

Then the judge read a statement from Father Castillo, who said that he had talked to Maxine and directed her to Tito's house. This was a major disappointment to Lorenzo, who had considered the priest an ally.

He knew what they said was true, and it was all very damaging to Maxine. She had lied to everyone she encountered. And, unstated at this point, was the fact that Tito was already in the U.S. He had already been taken by her. In her eyes, it had been for Tito's own good, but it would certainly be viewed here as kidnapping.

The last piece of evidence was a photo projected on a screen at the front of the courtroom. It showed Maxine and Tito standing in front of a sign that read, Oregon State Capitol.

This was the most damaging evidence of all. Lorenzo was impressed by the thoroughness of the investigation. He suddenly realized that it would be nearly impossible to gain Maxine's freedom in a conventional way.

The judge ordered Maxine to stand. "Maxine March, how do you plead?" he asked.

"*Inocente,*" she said tenuously, not forcefully as Lorenzo had recommended.

The judge turned to Lorenzo.

"*Señor* Madrid?"

Lorenzo stood as Maxine sat down and said, "At this point, we are not admitting that *Señorita* March took the boy from his home in Montecristi. In fact, she did not. How he wound up in the United States is unknown to me. We will show that she knew nothing about how he got to Oregon."

The judge waved his hand in dismissal and Lorenzo sat down. "Before I announce my decision, I must read to you the pertinent statute." He adjusted his glasses. Laura, the translator, again leaned in to interpret for Lorenzo. "Ecuador is party to the Hague Convention on Protection of Children and Cooperation in Respect of Intercountry Adoption. Pursuant to those requirements, Ecuadorian law does not allow an Ecuadorian child to travel to the United States to be adopted. Therefore, prospective adoptive parents must obtain a full and final adoption under Ecuadorian law before the child can emigrate to the United States to be adopted."

The judge removed his glasses and looked at Maxine. "Maxine March, you are hereby ordered to be held for trial in this court one month from today on the charge of kidnapping."

At that point, Maxine fainted, her shackles clanging as she slid off the chair to the floor.

27

THAD GOT TITO OUT OF BED and had him put on a sweatshirt and jeans. "We need to go downtown for a while, Tito. It's an adventure."

The boy's eyes sparkled. "Okay, *bueno. Pero uno problema, tio.*"

"And what is that?

"*Zapatos.* Shoes. I have no shoes."

They both laughed as Thad helped the boy put on his sneakers.

On the drive to the library, Thad called Nettles and asked him to meet them there.

"Why? What happened?" said Nettles. "Tell me!"

"I can't go into details now. Little ears are listening."

"Got it! I'll see you there."

They arrived at the library in ten minutes and found Jo sitting outside on a bench. Tito unbuckled himself, opened the door and ran to her. "Miss Jo, Miss Jo, I have missed you so much!" She picked him up and kissed him.

"Anything? Still missing?" Thad asked.

She nodded. And at that moment, Greg Nettles walked up to them. Thad shook his head. "Jo, maybe Tito would like to look at books in the children's section," he said.

"Good idea." She took the boy by the hand and led him inside. "I think you will enjoy looking for books we don't have at home," she said, as they disappeared inside.

"*Bueno,*" he said.

"So what's going on?" asked Greg.

Thad told him about Jo's call and her discovery of Sam's books and the spilled coffee upstairs.

"Let's have a look," said Greg as they both walked into the building and up the stairs.

Someone had wiped up the coffee and stacked Sam's notebook and the law books he had been reading. "Look at this," said Thad, as he picked up a tiny object from the chair Sam had probably been sitting on.

"Looks like an emblem of some kind," said Thad. "An eagle and some letters." He handed it to Nettles.

"Oh, God. MS-13."

28

AFTER LORENZO AND JENKINS REVIVED MAXINE, they helped her stand and walk back to the holding cell. At the doorway, a guard barred their entrance. "I'm talking to the judge right now," said Jenkins. "You need medical help." The guard helped her through the door.

"I'll be in touch," shouted Lorenzo as she disappeared inside.

By this time, Sebastión Blanco, the court administrator had reappeared. With the help of Laura, the interpreter, Jenkins insisted that Maxine have better treatment. At first, Blanco seemed bored as Jenkins talked about getting medical help and medicine for Maxine and better living conditions. "I must insist on behalf of my government that you help this woman, an American citizen!"

"What makes her so special?" said Blanco. "We have prisoners from many countries. What makes an American so much more important than them?"

At that moment, the door to the judge's chambers opened and the judge himself appeared in the doorway. He motioned for Blanco to approach. He walked over to the judge who quietly said a few words. Blanco nodded. He walked back to where Lorenzo and Jenkins were standing.

"I am to call the superintendent at Litoral," he said. "*Señorita* Marsh will be sent to the doctor at the prison and be kept in the clinic there until her trial." He turned and walked away, a scowl on his face.

"He doesn't like to be contradicted, even by a judge. But the judge does not want an American woman to die in one of their prisons," said Lorenzo. They stepped into the hall and turned to leave.

"Lorenzo. How wonderful to see you again." Margo Acosta was headed their way at a rapid pace. She kissed Lorenzo on both cheeks and her hug lasted a bit longer than necessary.

"And who is this handsome gentleman?" she said, turning to Jenkins.

"Kurt Jenkins of the American Embassy."

"Of course, how silly of me. I met you at the ambassador's garden party last summer."

"Of course."

"This is Margo Acosta, Kurt. She rescued me in Montecristi yesterday."

"A slight exaggeration, Lorenzo. I only offered you my hospitality for one night and you escaped without even saying goodbye."

"And what brings you to this courthouse?" asked Lorenzo.

"I am meeting an old friend for lunch," she said. "I came here to, how do you say it, kill some time. Will the two of you join me for lunch?

Lorenzo looked at his watch. "I need to get to the airport. My flight leaves in three hours. I will try to bring your dear friend Bobbi Bouquet with me when I return in several weeks."

"Wonderful. I'll make inquiries about the film festival."

He kissed her on both cheeks and turned to leave.

"*¡Chao!* My darling."

"Goodbye Margo."

As they walked away from her, Jenkins nudged Lorenzo in the ribs. "What's this 'my darling' stuff," he laughed.

Lorenzo just shook his head in dismay. "A very long story."

29

ALBERTO HAD A LONG FACE as he walked with Lorenzo to the departure gate. "I'll miss you, boss. Who else will keep things so exciting?"

"You've got a point there, Alberto. Try to behave yourself while I am away. I'll be back as soon as I can. Keep a low profile in case some of those MS-13 guys are looking for you. I've ask Kurt Jenkins to let you live in the embassy for a while. "

"Cool. Lots of good looking *señoritas* at the embassy."

"Just keep it zipped," laughed Lorenzo, indicating his crotch. "And your mouth too. We've got to keep all of this quiet. Okay?"

"*Sí, sí, sí*. No worries, boss. *Adiós*."

As Lorenzo walked to the gate, two men near the departure gate turned and left the building. If they were looking for Alberto, they didn't see him. He had grabbed a janitor's cap and was emptying trash at another gate.

▯ ▯ ▯ ▯ ▯

The flight back to Los Angeles was uneventful. Alex the steward was not on duty. The service was good but he did not say much to the people who attended him, nor to his seatmate, a young man preoccupied with playing games on his laptop. After dinner, he reclined his seat and went to sleep. He did not wake up until they were an hour from L.A.

The steward placed an elegant

breakfast of crepes, fruit and pastries in front of him. "Coffee," he said to the young man, "I really need that, thank you. It's been a great trip, even though I've slept a lot. I appreciate everything."

As he ate, Lorenzo thought about what he had to do to prepare for his return to Ecuador. Along with amassing and reading material to substantiate the case, he had to spend time with Tito and prepare him for a few more weeks without his "papa."

He also thought about how he would involve Bobbi Bouquet in his defense. He suspected that Margo Acosta was exerting influence behind the scenes. Why, he did not know. Resentment towards Maxine for taking the boy? Romantic entanglements with officials of a government her late husband was a part of? Sheer meddling by someone who had too much time on her hands? If he could secure her help by bringing Bobbi to Ecuador, it was a small price to pay. The time it would take to get her ready to play this role and to fend off her sexual advances to him would be worth it. What was it about him that attracted these older ladies? He guessed that his homosexuality was the biggest reason. They liked his looks and his personality but considered him someone they could convert. It was all pretty baffling but he planned to use it with Bobbi. He needed to see her as quickly as he could arrange a meeting.

Once he had cleared customs, he sat down at a Starbucks and tried to call Sam to say he was nearly home. When Sam didn't answer, he tried Thad, whose phone went to voice mail. Then Greg, whose secretary said he was out of the office on assignment. He left a message to say he was back in the country and would be in Oregon that night.

As he finished his coffee, Lorenzo decided to make another call. He consulted his contact list and punched in a number.

The call was answered on the third ring. "Bobbi Bouquet's residence. How may I help you?"

30

LORENZO DROVE HIS RENTAL CAR TO A FAMILIAR DESTINATION: Bobbi Bouquet's rented house just off San Vicente in Santa Monica. He had gone through the ornate gates a year or so ago to convince her to star in the movie he had been tricked into producing. During the course of filming on location in Oregon, they had become friends. Some in the business would call Bobbi a has-been, but to Lorenzo, she was still a star in the old meaning of that word. She represented the old-fashioned glamour he loved seeing in movies as a young poor kid growing up in the barrio of East L.A. Then, it was a world he could only dream about, but now he was a part of it. No more pressing his nose against the window of opportunity. He had achieved more in life than he ever thought he could.

He drove up the driveway towards a large mansion, but turned left down a wide road to the smaller house where she actually lived. Still a star, but a star living in more modest circumstances than she preferred. He had barely gotten out of the car when she rushed down the steps and threw her arms around him.

"Lorenzo, my darling! How good it is to see you and have you in my arms!" Lorenzo hugged her back, trying not to pull away from her tight embrace but finding it difficult to breathe. "My astrologer told me you would come back to me. I prayed for it, although I'm not a religious person, as you of all people know. Come in, come in. We'll have coffee or tea or,

what was that old book title about airline stewardesses, ME? Ha, ha, ha!"

They entered the hall and walked down into the elegant living room, the walls of which were covered with large photos and paintings of Bobbi in various roles.

As always she was dressed in a long silk caftan. Her hair and makeup had been perfectly applied and the result took years off her actual age. Lorenzo had looked it up and she was 75. She looked 50.

After a maid had brought in a tray of coffee and croissants, Bobbi sat down next to Lorenzo on the couch and snuggled into his shoulder. "My, how I've missed these tender moments with you," she said.

My how your memory is failing you, he thought to himself. In actuality, there were no tender moments. He had spent much of the time with her on the set trying to get her to learn her lines and be on time. She was difficult, and gloried in being difficult. She was, after all, a star. Really a former star, but no one would dare say that. "Bobbi, I need to get right to the point. I'm between planes but I couldn't miss the chance to see you again and also to make you a proposition, a business proposition."

"Oh shoot," she smiled. "I was hoping for another kind of proposition. Ha, ha, ha!" She got up and moved to a nearby chair, refilling their cups on the way. "Okay, let's have it!"

"Do you remember working with a young actress, years ago, named Margo Acosta?"

"My darling, do you realize how many actors and actresses I have worked with on all the films I have done? You've seen my list of credits. I can't recall all the people on the film we did together last year, let alone someone from that many years ago."

"She is from Ecuador but was in the U.S. for a while and got a role in *The Bride Wore Blood*."

Bobbi thought for a moment. "Was she from a convent, maybe?"

"Yes, I think she mentioned that."

"I do remember her because she was so young and innocent. I could see something of myself in her, like when I started out. Why do you ask?"

"I encountered her in Ecuador, where I have been working on a case. I had the occasion to visit her home in the countryside near Quito. She took me on a tour and when we got to her library, I was amazed to see publicity photos of you and a few posters about your movies."

"How charming," said Bobbi. "One does not find true fans very often. But what does this have to do with me?"

"Bear with me and I will give you some background." For the next half hour, Lorenzo told Bobbi the story of Maxine and Tito and how Maxine had been imprisoned when she went to Ecuador to try to adopt him. He went over his trip to Montecristi and about encountering her fan, Margo Acosta. And also about Maxine's upcoming trial for kidnapping.

"What does this woman have to do with your client."

"I am not certain, but I think it is because of a misplaced sense of patriotism. No one should take away—or kidnap, if you will— 'one of our children,' even if the boy was an orphan living on the streets. Also, because of her late husband's various positions in the government, she is well-connected. She has made it her mission to make sure Maxine pays for this alleged crime."

"But you still have not told me about my involvement," she said, tapping her fingers on the arm of the chair in impatience.

"Okay, here is what I want to hire you to do."

"Hire? I like the sound of that," said Bobbi.

"Since Margo idolizes you, I proposed that she organize a film festival featuring you and your films—a film festival in Quito. She said you have a big fan base there."

"I do get fan mail from all the Latin American countries to this day. I think the studios send my movies to theaters down there to make money. I even get a tiny share of the sales. Very tiny."

"So this interests you?"

"I don't yet know enough to be interested or not be interested, my darling."

"Here's my plan, which I have told only to you at this point. I think I will lose this case. I hate to be so pessimistic but I must be a realist. I'm afraid I can't keep Maxine March out of prison. I may have to break her out of prison."

Bobbi looked surprised. "I don't know you very well, but I think of you as more cerebral than a man of action, at least in the way you seem to be proposing."

"Yeah, that is me, but I am desperate. I need to return Maxine to the little boy, who I have been caring for. I have grown to love him, but I must go against my own wishes and do what's right."

"If you were married, you could have a kid of your own, or do that even if you aren't married. I've never wanted children. My career came first, as I suppose yours has. I am not sorry."

"And neither am I," he said.

"I am intrigued by your idea and honored that you think I can help," she said. "I am getting old . . . don't tell anyone I ever said that! I will deny it! How can I help?"

"I propose that we use your fame as a diversion. Using this woman's devotion to you, we will set up a film festival in Quito and then do another one at the prison. It is near the Peruvian border, and if things go badly at Maxine's trial, I will get her out from there."

"Leaving me to face the music?" she said, matter of factly.

"NEVER! I will have military professionals helping me, I mean special forces commandos. We will not leave without you. I promise you that."

"Do I get paid for this adventure? I am still a working girl, you know, with lots of expenses."

"I will negotiate a fee for you from Margo Acosta, who is very wealthy. Your expenses will be paid, including first class plane fare and a suite in a first class hotel. I will pay you $10,000 when this mission is over."

"I like calling it that," she said, "a mission, like in one of my films, *Moscow Undercover,* but in Latin America instead of Russia."

"Exactly like that," he said. "So you are in?"

"Lorenzo, my darling, have I ever been able to refuse you?"

31

AS SOON AS LORENZO HAD DRIVEN OUT THE GATES OF BOBBI'S ESTATE, he remembered all the calls he had placed without luck at the airport. He pulled over and checked his phone. Two from Thad, three from Greg but none from Sam. He tried Thad first since his family was living with him.

"You have reached the . . ." He disconnected.

Greg was next. "God, Lorenzo, where have you been? You were due back here yesterday!"

"I decided to see someone here in L.A. I need for the case. She is . . ."

"I don't care! Lorenzo, Sam is missing! Has been for two days!"

"Sam? Missing? Is Tito okay?"

"Yes, to all those questions."

"Tell me what happened." Lorenzo put the call on speaker phone so he could drive to the airport as he listened. Greg gave him a rundown of the circumstances of Sam's disappearance.

"Sounds like a professional job, obvi- ously to make a point with me," he said. "If they were trying to get my attention, they got it! They're messing with my household." He drove in silence for a few minutes.

"Lorenzo! Are you still there?"

"Yeah, I'm here."

"Could there be any connection to

your case?"

"I don't see how. Why would people here in the U.S. care about a court case in Ecuador? It doesn't make any sense."

"Something else I forgot to mention."

"What?"

"On Sam's chair at the law library, I found a small medallion with a logo marked MS-13. Have you heard of them?"

"Oh, yes, I have—and recently. That's the abbreviation for *Mara Salvatrucha*, that murderous gang that started in L.A. and now terrorizes countries all over Central America."

"You said, 'recently'?"

"A bunch of them ambushed me in Ecuador a few days ago and tried to kill me and my driver. This is beginning to make sense. Several years ago I helped you find the head of the drug gang in Oregon. These guys still blame me for his death. They are still reaching out to get me for that! God! I'm putting everyone I love in danger!"

"You helped me, Lorenzo," said Greg. "That's why I'm in this with you. Get back home! In the meantime, we're looking for Sam. I've got Oregon State Police on it. Since Thad's an assistant AG, that part was easy. They're watching his house. Tito and Jo are safe." By this time, Lorenzo had turned onto I-10.

"Lorenzo, I've gotta go!"

"One more thing, Greg. We really need Perez on this."

"That's what I was thinking."

32

ESTEBAN PEREZ HAD BEEN IN AND OUT OF LORENZO'S LIFE for several years. He had first met him several years before as a member of the drug gang that had captured him and tried to kill him, first in Oregon and later in L.A. He had arranged for his kidnapping and abduction to an isolated ranch in Southern Oregon. When Greg and a force of DEA agents raided the ranch, the leader of the cartel had been killed. Perez had escaped, but later turned up in L.A., still looking to avenge the death of his boss.

His plans to run the West Coast operation were thwarted by the arrival of Pantera, a vicious member of MS-13, complete with tattoos on his face and everywhere else on his body. Perez grew to hate Pantera as much as he hated Lorenzo. After the gang captured Lorenzo again, Pantera ordered Perez to shoot Lorenzo in the head. As he stood with a gun to Lorenzo's head, Perez turned and shot Pantera between the eyes. He told Lorenzo to run and he did.

A year or so later, Greg Nettles asked Lorenzo for his help in getting Perez to testify before a grand jury in return for his admittance to the Witness Protection Program. They met and shook hands and mended their differences. Perez was grateful to Lorenzo for reuniting him with his son. He pledged his willingness to help Lorenzo whenever he needed him.

Now seemed to be that time. Perez's connections to his old compatriots would probably help find Sam and who was after Lorenzo, yet another time.

□ □ □ □ □

Lorenzo called Greg and Thad as soon as he landed in Portland. He headed straight for Salem to see Tito. Both Greg and Thad promised to meet him at Thad's. And two Oregon State Police troopers got out as he approached their car which was parked in front of Thad's house. "Are you Lorenzo Madrid?"

"Yes, officer, I am."

"Go right in. Mr. Sampson notified us you'd be coming. The boy and his tutor are in the living room. Are you his dad?"

"Not exactly, at least not yet. It's complicated."

"Bright little kid. He does look like you. That's why I asked."

"Thanks, sergeant, I appreciate you guys being here. I hope we can figure out who is threatening me and my family so you can go home to yours."

Lorenzo walked in the front door and saw Jo and Tito sitting at a table. Tito was writing in a workbook of some kind with his back to the doorway. Jo saw Lorenzo and started to open her mouth but he put a finger to his lips. He crept up behind the boy and put both hands over his eyes. "What is this?" said the startled boy.

"It's your papa!" Tito whirled around and flung himself at Lorenzo. Both of them started to cry, joined soon by Jo.

"You are back to me! My papa, my papa! I thought you had left me forever!"

"I would never leave you, little man, never in a hundred years!" Lorenzo reached over and hugged Jo.

"Maybe it should be a thousand years! We have been learning numbers," cried Tito.

Lorenzo and Jo laughed. "I'm glad to see you using what I've taught you," said Jo.

"How can I thank you for taking such good care of my boy?" said Lorenzo, squeezing her hand.

She mouthed the word, "Sam?"

He shook his head. "Not yet. Greg is working on it. We've got some ideas."

At that point, both Thad and Greg entered the room. "Boy, are we glad to see you," said Thad, who hugged Lorenzo in a tight embrace. "We're doing fine here, but it will be much better now that you're here. Right Tito?"

"Yes, sir. *Señor* Thad. He is my new best friend, papa."

"What about me?" asked Greg, a dejected look on his face.

"And me, as well," said Jo, looking equally distressed.

For a moment Tito looked as if he couldn't decide, then his face brightened. "You are all *mis amigos!*"

"Yay!" they shouted.

"I hate to ruin this wonderful scene, but I need for us to talk, Lorenzo," said Greg.

"Go back to your lessons for a few minutes, Tito, and then you and I can have a talk."

"Okay, papa." He turned to Jo. "I know how to multiply and divide, Miss Jo."

"Oh you do, do you, you little scamp. Let's see if you really do."

As they left the room, Lorenzo heard Tito say, "What's a scamp?"

In the dining room, Greg brought the two of them up to date on the search for Sam. "There's not much to report," he said. "He was seen getting into a dark-colored sedan parked near the library. Two men were on either side of him. He was not struggling, according to two ladies who were walking their dogs. That's it. He vanished. I've reached out to my sources here and in Portland and no one knows anything."

"Perez? Did you contact him?"

"Not yet."

"Who is Perez?" asked Thad.

The two of them looked at one another and Greg nodded. "Esteban Perez is an enemy turned friend," said Lorenzo. He's a gang banger who once tried to kill me. But he has a soft spot and that soft spot involves his son, a boy about Tito's age."

"Perez contacted me last year and said he would become a witness before a grand jury investigating the drug gangs in the state," said Nettles. "He would do it on two conditions: that Lorenzo become involved and that we reunited him with his son and his mother. We agreed at once, he testified, and we got him into the Witness Protection Program."

"He promised to help me anytime I needed him," continued Lorenzo. "And he did last year at the coast."

"I know where he is, and I can get him to help us now," said Greg. "He still maintains contacts with his old friends in the gang, ones who don't know he ratted them out."

"If this does involve MS-13, will he have any contacts there?" asked Lorenzo

"Remember, that lunatic Pantera was from MS-13, although we didn't know what that was at the time," said Greg.

"MS-13? Jesus! Those guys are bad news!" said Thad. "I've seen lots of intelligence about them. We're poised for them to set up business in Oregon."

"Two things make us wonder about their involvement," said Greg. "One, they went after Lorenzo in Ecuador."

"Shit!" said Thad. "Not really!"

"Two, I found one of their medallions on a chair in the library where Sam was taken."

"Not good news!"

"We've got to get Perez's help," said Lorenzo. "He's the only one to help us find Sam and get them off my back."

"I've placed a call to a friend in the Marshal's Service," said Greg. "They handle people in Witness Protection. I think Perez is in Washington state somewhere. I'll try to set up a meeting."

"The sooner the better. I've got to prepare for Maxine's trial in Ecuador and set up some aspects of that."

"What aspects?" asked Nettles. "Wait, I don't think I want to know."

33

ALTHOUGH ESTEBAN PEREZ WAS HAPPY TO BE SETTLED IN A NEW TOWN and a new house, he missed his old life in some ways. He and his son and mother were safe now, true. But life was kind of boring. He had quit drinking so did not go to bars. He had taken a break from women, especially the prostitutes he had grown addicted to. He hoped to settle down some day with a decent woman. Someone who would love Rafael and tolerate his sometimes overbearing mother. That day would come.

In the meantime, he read a lot and tried to help his son with his homework. He enrolled in an "English as a Second Language" course at the local community college. His teacher said he was improving. Since he had loved fast cars all his life and dreamed of a job repairing them, he also signed up for an auto mechanics course—a pretty odd career goal for a former hit man, he often thought.

This somewhat peaceful life had been interrupted by Greg Nettles's call. When he explained what had happened to Lorenzo and his family, Perez asked a few questions then said, "I'm in."

It took only a few hours to arrange for vacation days from his job as a clerk in an auto store. He had been there a year so was entitled to two weeks off with pay. He called his aunt and uncle to come from New Mexico to stay with his mother and son. Greg promised to ask the Marshal's Service to check on them from time to time.

The day after Greg called, a package arrived containing $5,000 in cash and a bus ticket. "You're in the sticks so far that it seemed easier for you to get here by bus than go to Seattle to catch a plane." Good thinking. Greg said he or one of his men would pick him up at the main bus station in Portland the next afternoon.

Perez packed some clothes and got his Glock pistol out of the safe he kept it in. He was ready.

❏ ❏ ❏ ❏ ❏

Greg was waiting at the bus station in Portland—a seedy terminal like every city seemed to have.

"Perez," said Nettles, "thanks for coming." They shook hands and walked to the car, double parked on the street because of the official license plate on his car. "How ya doing, Perez? Life okay for you and your family?"

"Yes, Agent Nettles, it is as good as it can be under the circumstances. Beats prison, I guess. I made my decision to go into the life a long time ago. I was a dumb fucking kid who got talked into it by his friends. Lots of money, lots of girls, lots of action. Really dumb. I'm lucky to be alive, I guess."

Nettles didn't say anything for a few miles as they headed south on I-5, because Perez was being talkative and Nettles didn't want to interrupt him. It seemed like Perez needed to talk. "You know, agent, it feels real weird to be riding in a government car with you, without me in the backseat behind a screen wearing handcuffs."

"I'll bet it does."

"So tell me what this is all about."

"Your friend Lorenzo is in the middle of an international adoption case. He has been in Ecuador preparing for the trial of an American woman who is accused of kidnapping a local kid."

"Was that the boy I saw at that lighthouse on the coast a few months ago?"

"The very same, yes."

"I thought he was Lorenzo's kid."

"No, he's been taking care of him because the American woman, name of Maxine March, asked him to. He has been helped by a lady tutor and his paralegal, a Black kid named Sam. It is Sam that we are worried about."

"How come?"

"He disappeared from the law library in Salem last night. And on the chair where he had been sitting was this." He handed Perez the emblem.

"MS-13. *Dios mío!* Not good news. They are killers, no doubt about it. I know all about them. The dude I killed a year or so ago in L.A., Pantera, was one of them. More deadly than the worst snake. This means they're coming into the Pacific Northwest and are after Lorenzo."

"They blame him for the death of the boss—your boss—in the desert," said Nettles. "

"I blamed him too until I found out the truth. This is very bad!" At that moment, Greg guided the car into the driveway of Thad's house. Lorenzo came bounding out the door. "We meet again, counselor," Perez said warily.

"Thank you for coming, Esteban. We need your help." They stood facing one another awkwardly for a few seconds more. Then Lorenzo embraced Perez and the former gang banger hugged him back.

34

LORENZO WALKED NETTLES AND PEREZ INTO THAD'S STUDY, a book-lined room off the hall. Here they could talk without anyone overhearing them, especially Tito who was already asking questions about his pal, Sam. As soon as these two left, Lorenzo needed to spend time with the boy.

"*Dios mío!*" said Perez, his eyes virtually bugging out of his head. "Have you read all of these books?"

"These aren't my books. This is the house of my friend, Thad Sampson."

"He's probably got just as many," said Nettles.

"Sit down, please," said Lorenzo. "So what do you think, Esteban? Who took Sam?"

"I called around."

"You are free to make calls even though you're in witness protection?" asked Greg. "I thought you were cut off from the world, I mean, your old world."

"Yes and no," said Perez. "There are ways, especially when there is an important reason to do that. And this is important. I want to help you guys anytime I can."

"Thank you a lot," said Lorenzo.

"You were saying about the calls?" said Greg.

"Sure, the calls. I know a few guys around here who are in touch with the

various gangs that come through Oregon. They told me that a few members of MS-13 have come to this state to find and kill you, Lorenzo."

Lorenzo's face turned pale and he took a deep breath. "God, that's all I need. They still blame me for Robles's death."

Perez nodded. "I was there, but I didn't pull the trigger. He had tried to bury me alive, for God's sake!"

"One of my men did it, as I recall," said Nettles.

"And also Pantera. They say you need to answer for Pantera."

"Perez, you're the one who shot him in the head, for God's sake!"

He turned to Nettles. "You didn't hear that, Greg. Pantera was a truly evil man who deserved to die, as painfully as possible."

"Esteban and I talked about that long ago," said Nettles. "It's not a problem."

"Back to Sam," said Lorenzo, impatiently.

"They picked him up to get to you, after their attempt to kill you in Ecuador did not work out."

"So it **was** them."

"MS-13 has a long reach," explained Perez. "They're in all the South American countries now."

"So I've heard," said Lorenzo.

"You'd better believe it," added Greg. "Now I guess they're going to be a problem for me here in Oregon."

"So what can you tell us about Sam?" said Lorenzo.

"My friends tell me he's being held somewhere in the coastal mountains," said Perez. "Maybe that place where you were working on that movie a year or more ago. You know, that place where crazy people used to be."

"The sanitarium?" said Lorenzo, pausing to think. "I guess that makes sense. Nobody goes there. It's falling apart, even though we rebuilt some of it for that movie. They could slip in and out of there without attracting too much attention."

"How'd they find out about it?" asked Greg.

Perez looked embarrassed. "I'm afraid from me," he said. "After I went out there to talk to you, I told an old *amigo,* about it. Mostly what it had been and that some people think it is haunted by ghosts. I guess he told other guys and they told MS-13 guys. I am sorry."

"It wasn't your fault," said Lorenzo.

"Yeah, but it was kinda' stupid," said Greg, an edge in his voice.

"Perez's eyes flashed in anger. I said I was sorry."

Lorenzo glared at Greg, as if to warn him not to go into that subject any further. "How could you know," he said to Perez. "The main thing is to use your knowledge to find Sam and get him out of there. Right, Greg?"

"Yeah, sure. Sorry, Esteban."

"Okay by me," he shrugged.

"How do we make sure Sam is there?" said Lorenzo.

"From what my friend told me, he is there. I will go there and look around."

"But that'll take a lot of time," said Lorenzo.

"Time we may not have," said Greg. "How long before they kill him?"

"Only a day or two."

"Wait a minute," said Lorenzo. "How can they act so fast when they haven't even contacted me with their demands?"

"My friend gave me this," said Perez, handing Lorenzo a piece of paper.

"God, Perez, why didn't you say so before!" said Nettles angrily.

"Just calm down, Greg," said Lorenzo. "Let me read what they say."

He unfolded the paper. "Oh God!" he handed the page to Greg who said, "Shit!"

Lorenzo took it back and looked at it again. It was a photo of Sam, his mouth duct taped, his eyes full of fear. A black hood had been pulled up onto his forehead, as if to show his face to the camera before the hood was pulled down again. His face was covered with dark bruises and one eye was swollen and purple.

"Poor Sam," said Lorenzo. "See what happens to people I get close to? We've got to get him out of there, even if I have to offer myself in his place. I can't have his death on my conscience!"

"What's this **we** business?" said Greg. "You're not going anywhere near that place!"

"You want to bet?"

Perez turned to Greg. "It might work better if Lorenzo does go and we show him to them," he said.

"Like a decoy," said Lorenzo, nodding his head. "A good idea, Esteban."

"Well, I don't like it," said Greg. "You're not trained. You don't know how to use a gun. The liability if something happened to you would be horrendous! Not to mention that my career in law enforcement would end right there."

"I'm going, Greg, whether you like it or not!"

"Okay, okay. I'll loan you a bullet-proof vest at the very least."

"I suggest we go there tonight," said Perez. "They're still getting things set up. They won't expect us."

"Okay, then, we'll do it tonight," said Greg. "Perez and I will go to my office and I can call in my most trusted agents. I can also introduce you to my guys so they won't shoot you by mistake."

"Don't I know all about that kind of mistake," said Perez, grimly.

They agreed to meet at 9 p.m. and drive to the sanitarium.

◻ ◻ ◻ ◻ ◻

When Nettles and Perez left the house, Lorenzo went to find Tito and Jo. "There are my two favorite people," he said, as he entered the living room.

"Papa, you are here by my side," yelled Tito as he raced across the room and jumped into Lorenzo's outstretched arms. He

143

couldn't resist giving him several kisses.

"You're getting to be so big, pretty soon you won't want kisses."

"I always want kisses from you," said Tito. "You are my papa!"

Jo smiled, but had a sad look on her face.

"Sit down, both of you," Lorenzo said. They did, Jo on a couch and Lorenzo on a chair, with Tito squirming up onto his lap.

"I have to go out again tonight, Tito. But I promise to be here in the morning and fix you pancakes for breakfast." Although the boy usually reacted with enthusiasm at that news, he just moved even closer to Lorenzo. "I thought you'd be jumping for joy at that news."

Tito looked perplexed. "How can I jump for joy, papa? I like to jump, but how do I find this 'joy' to jump for?"

Both Lorenzo and Jo smiled. "It's what we say and do when we're happy, darlin' boy," said Jo.

"Tell me what you and Jo have been studying."

The boy perked up at the question and began telling Lorenzo all about dinosaurs and whales and addition and subtraction. "I now write my name in *Ingles* and even longer things like . . ."

"Sentences," said Jo.

"Sentences," repeated Tito.

"That **is** good news," said Lorenzo. "You can write me a letter when I'm gone and tell me . . ."

"Why do I write to you, papa," chuckled Tito. "You are here by my side."

"True, but I mean when I am away for just a little while." He held up one hand and brought a thumb and forefinger so they were about a half inch apart. Tito yawned.

"I think it's time for good boys to be in bed," said Jo.

Tito jumped down from Lorenzo's lap and kissed him. "Good night, little man. "I'll see you in the morning at pancake time."

"Pancakes, pancakes, pancakes," yelled Tito as he marched from the room.

"Go on in and fetch your pajamas," said Jo. "I'll be right there to help you with your bath." She walked to the door with Lorenzo. "Does this have anything to do with Sam," she whispered.

"Yeah, it does. We're pretty sure we know where they're holding him. Now, we just have to go there and get him out."

"You're going to be where there might be guns?"

Lorenzo nodded. "Afraid so."

"Heaven help us," she said. "I'll pray for you and everyone else involved here."

"I've got to go. Thank you for all you do for Tito and for all of us." He hugged her and turned, grabbed a warm jacket and cap and picked up a small duffle and left the house.

Trite but true, the die was cast.

35

THINGS HAD BEEN A BIT BETTER FOR MAXINE since she returned from Quito. By order of the judge, she was now living not in a cell but an actual room in the main building of the prison. A local doctor had been in once but did not seem to know all that much about medicine. Thanks to the intervention of Gustavo, Dawn was permitted to visit her every other day. Sandra was deemed too rambunctious to be allowed out of the secure area.

"How ya doin', baby?" Dawn asked. "You sleeping better? You look good. The color's back in your cheeks."

The truth was, Maxine did not look well at all. She had lost so much weight, her clothes hung on her thin frame like a scarecrow in a field. Despite the foul tasting cough syrup she took twice a day, she coughed all the time. Unfortunately, the doctor ignored her questions about that and listened only to her heart and not her lungs the one time he came.

"Let me see if they'll let me take you outside for some fresh air," said Dawn. She walked to the door and asked to see Gustavo, who was now in charge of this part of the prison. He came to the door quickly.

"*Señorita* Dawn. *Buenos días.* What can I do for you today?"

She pulled him out into the hall and whispered, "Maxine looks bad. I think she has TB. You know TB?"

He nodded. "Tuberculosis." He pointed to his chest. "Bad lungs."

"Exactly. She needs fresh air and fruit and soup. And tea, lots of tea. Can we walk out into the garden?"

"Of course," he said. "I was told to keep her comfortable." He leaned over and whispered, "The authorities do not want her too sick to go on trial, I think. Bad, how do you say it, PR?"

They both walked into Maxine's room. She was sitting in the only chair and staring into space.

"Buenos días, Señorita Maxina," he said softly. *"Cómo está usted?"*

"Good morning, Gustavo. It is always good to see you. I have a new name. *Maxina.* I like it. I have never liked 'Maxine.' Too boring and old-fashioned."

"We get to go outside to the garden, honey," said Dawn. "Gustavo is the boss here now and he said it is okay."

"It would be nice to get out of this room," she said, wearily. "The walls start closing in after a while."

"Put on this sweatshirt and we can go now."

Maxine stood up and seemed to wobble on her legs for a second before Dawn grabbed her arm and helped her finish dressing. She also combed her hair. "There you go," she said. "Ready for the outside world."

The three of them walked down the hall and out the open door to the garden. As soon as the sunlight touched her face, Maxine smiled. She took a deep breath. "Smell that air. It's wonderful."

36

IT HAD TAKEN ONLY THREE HOURS FOR GREG TO ASSEMBLE HIS MEN.
Fifteen of them were now spread out in the woods around the sanitarium's main building. Lorenzo suspected that Sam was being held in the large room housing the hot springs. Like in the days when this was a well-known and fashionable medical facility, this is where the treatments took place. Tubs were filled with scalding water and the patients were made to sit in them until they passed out. In theory, they emerged either cured of venereal disease or TB, or they convulsed until they died. This would be a perfect place for the MS-13 goons to frighten Sam to death or kill him and easily dispose of his body in one of the tubs or the hot spring itself.

As Lorenzo and Greg waited in the nearby wood, one of his men crept up to the window and looked in. He turned and ran to them. "Black guy?"

"Yeah, that's Sam."

"He's in there tied up with a collar around his neck. A chain hooked to it is hooked to the wall."

"God, what a nightmare for Sam," said Lorenzo. "I'm feeling really guilty right now."

"No time for that, Lorenzo," said Nettles. "We've got to move." Perez walked over to them but said nothing.

"Ready?" said Nettles, looking at Perez.

"Ready for what?" asked Lorenzo. "You guys have cooked something up without telling me."

"Those guys in there are my former *compadres*, said Perez. "They know me and will listen to me when I tell them to leave you alone. I'll tell them I killed Pantera."

"That will be suicide," said Lorenzo. "You can't do it. I won't let you. You're back with your son and in a new life. I'll do this. I'll go in there and try to reason with them. I caused this mess."

"You're not a professional, Lorenzo," said Greg. "Trust me, you're better off as an observer."

Lorenzo's eyes flashed in the dark. Breaking away from them quickly, he rushed towards the building and broke a window with the butt of the gun Greg had given him. Greg cursed, then signaled his men to follow Lorenzo. One of them ignited a grenade and the billowing smoke wafted quickly around the large room, mixing with the steam from the springs.

The two men guarding Sam had been asleep, leaning against one of the tubs. As they jerked up and reached from their guns, shots rang out from the other side of the room as Greg's men advanced. Both thugs fell where they stood. As he raced to Sam's side, Lorenzo noticed a tall man standing on a balcony high above. His face and bare chest were covered with the tattoos members of MS-13 favored. The man aimed his pistol and fired. Lorenzo fell to the ground.

37

KURT JENKINS WAS IMPRESSED BY THE IMPROVEMENT in Maxine's surroundings as he sat in the garden where they had met before. The judge's order to move her here and see to her medical needs was a sign that the Ecuadorian government was concerned about this case. This was both good and bad. The good came in the improvement of her treatment and the scheduling of her trial fairly quickly. He had known of drug cases involving American citizens where the trial was held a year after their arrest. The bad was the attention and the charge. How could people in Ecuador not be incensed at what, in their eyes, was the kidnapping of a little boy? He had to agree with that sentiment. In this case, however, it wasn't true. The kid was an orphan and would probably be dead had he not been taken to the U.S.

A door opened and Maxine walked into the garden, helped by another woman dressed in prison clothes. Maxine looked bad, pale and hunched over and shaking. She coughed into a handkerchief from time to time.

"It's okay, baby," said the woman. "We'll sit you down over here to talk to your friend."

She turned and offered a calloused hand. "Dawn Young. I'm Maxine's nurse and protector."

"Kurt Jenkins from the embassy."

"I'm gonna' leave you here with Mr. Jenkins but I'll be right outside that door

over there. Okay?" As she passed Jenkins she whispered, "She's getting worse every day."

Jenkins sat next to Maxine. "How are you doing?"

"I'm okay, I guess," she replied in a voice so faint Jenkins had to lean closer to hear her. "This is a much better place. Did you arrange this? If you did, I thank you very much."

"It was that judge. I don't think the government here wants the bad publicity of putting a woman on trial who has been mistreated." She coughed again and Jenkins saw blood on the handkerchief. "You okay? You want me to call your friend or the doctor?"

"No, that's okay. I'm used to it. The medicine worked at first, but it doesn't seem to do much good now." She paused and ran her hands over her face and her hair. "I'm sure I'm a mess. They gave me better clothes than before but I look like a scarecrow in them. I've lost a lot of weight."

"You look fine."

"So how's my case going? Lorenzo has gone back to Oregon I imagine."

"I haven't heard from him, but I know he is working hard to get ready for your trial."

Maxine started crying. "Trial! I'm being put on trial for saving a little boy! It isn't fair! And I wasn't the one who took him! Someone else started this whole mess! It wasn't me!"

She was sobbing so much that the straitlaced and formal Kurt Jenkins felt compelled to put his arm around her. "I don't know Lorenzo well, but I think he will do all he can to free you."

"You don't know that!" she said between sobs.

Jenkins handed her his handkerchief. "Thanks," she sniffled.

She dried her eyes. Jenkins moved to a chair opposite her. "I don't know what Lorenzo's strategy will be. Sympathy maybe? Love of the boy and the desire to protect him?"

Maxine looked him squarely in the face. "But I was not the one who took him! Did you know that? Paul Bickford did!"

"He's the Special Ops guy who you were married to?"

"Oh no, we were never married. Lovers for a while, yes, but married, no! He's the kind of guy who's married to the Army."

"So how did he get involved with the boy?"

"He rescued me from some bad guys who were after me in Montecristi where I was on assignment helping a friend. When Paul came to get me, he met Tito and fell in love with him. In all the time I've known him, he's only loved the Army, never me or another human being as far as I know. But he took to the boy. I'll never forget the scene when we had to leave Tito. As the helicopter lifted off, there was Tito on the ground crying his eyes out."

At the memory, she started crying again and then said, "Paul returned, took Tito, and arranged for him to be sent to me in the U.S."

"So you really did not have anything to do with the actual removing of the boy from Ecuador?"

"No. I did not!"

"Does Lorenzo know this?"

"Yes, I told him everything a long time ago."

"I'm no lawyer but that seems like it would bolster your case."

"Yes, it probably would. If Paul would testify, that would be even better."

"Maybe Lorenzo has plans to find him and involve him in the case."

"No chance of that, I'm sure," she said. "Ever since I've known him, he has had a habit of disappearing when things get tough. I'm sure he's off on some mysterious mission. He's forgotten me and Tito long ago."

"I'm not so sure," said Jenkins. He moved next to her and whispered, "He tried to save you at the prison. He and some of his men tried to break you out last month."

"WHAT? I can't believe it! Really? What happened?"

"Someone tipped off the prison authorities and they ambushed him when he got outside. There was a gunfight and . . ."

"And Paul was killed?"

Before Jenkins could explain, Maxine collapsed and fell sideways. Dawn and the friendly guard Gustavo rushed out and carried her back inside.

IN THE CONFUSION AND THE BILLOWING SMOKE, Nettles pulled Lorenzo out of the way, unsure if he was alive or dead. Shots rang out from all directions indicating that the gang members were scattered around this part of the building. He stood up and signaled for his men to move in and locate the shooters. When they saw him, the gang members started shooting at him. He easily ducked the bullets and soon heard the groans from those hit by his team members.

He looked up at the balcony and did not see the tattooed leader at first. He seemed to be having trouble reloading his rifle. As the gang leader tried to get it to function, Perez crept up behind him and slit his throat.

Nettles blinked at the suddenness of the move, and its finality. No need for a trial here or imprisonment for a guy who civilized society would not miss.

Perez walked to the edge of the balcony and gave a thumbs-up sign as he wiped blood off the blade of his knife.

Lorenzo groaned and Nettles moved over to him. "Lorenzo, Lorenzo. Are you with us, buddy?"

He opened his eyes. "Where else would I be?"

They both laughed. "Where were you hit?"

Lorenzo pointed to his right shoulder.

"Here, I think."

"Good thing you were wearing that Kevlar vest. You'll live."

Lorenzo tried to stand but could not get to his feet on his own. "Easy, easy. You still took a heavy shock."

"What about me? I've got to be in super shock," said a voice.

"SAM!" they shouted. Two of Greg's men had untied Sam and were helping him to his feet. He limped over to them.

"Come here," said Lorenzo. "You deserve at least a hug."

"Thanks, boss. Sorry to cause all this trouble."

"Don't be crazy. You risked your life for us!"

"How do you feel, Sam? Did they hurt you at all?"

"Not really. They roughed me up a lot at first, but seemed intent on getting you to come after me so they could kill you. From what I could make out with my limited understanding of Spanish, they hate you. Is everything okay at home, I mean at Thad's house?"

"Everything is fine. The little man misses you a lot."

"I hate to break up this happy scene but my man Napolitano is a trained medic. I want him to look at both of you."

A young DEA agent stepped forward and directed Lorenzo to sit down. He took off Lorenzo's vest and t-shirt and began to press and prod the wound. "Does this hurt, sir?"

"No. Just a little."

"This?" Lorenzo shook his head.

He probed more, this time putting on more pressure. "This?"

"No."

"Okay, great. The bullet didn't puncture the vest. There's not much damage that I can detect. I'm going to give you a shot of antibiotics just in case. You should see your doctor soon, though."

"Good news," said Lorenzo. "Thanks. It doesn't even hurt."

"Here's the bullet," said another of Greg's men. "It hit this railing when it glanced off his vest."

"Preserve it," said Nettles, "although I don't think there'll be any blowback over any of this. We broke up a gang of MS-13 bastards. No questions will be asked by anyone."

"How many bodies?" asked Nettles.

"Six including the tall dude with all the tattoos."

"*El Gato,* the cat," said Perez. "He was the new boss here in Oregon. Very bad *hombre.* Very bad." He turned to Lorenzo. "He may not be the last to come for you. These guys have long memories."

"Yeah, I guess," said Lorenzo. "But I'm not going to give up all the things I value in life because I'm afraid."

He turned to Nettles. "Can we get out of here?"

Nettles nodded and conferred with his men about calling for a van to transport the bodies to the morgue in Salem. "I'll drive my friends back to town and start the paperwork."

◻ ◻ ◻ ◻ ◻

At Thad's house, Sam ran to the front door but Lorenzo hung back to talk to Nettles and Perez. "Some day, I'll be able to do something for you. You guys have saved my ass more than I care to remember."

He turned to Perez. "Will you go back to wherever you live now?"

"I have no choice, Lorenzo. But I feel safe there and I have my son and my mother with me. I owe the both of you for my life. This is, how do you say it, a two way street."

The three hugged one another, Perez more tentative than the others. Lorenzo guessed that hugging another man was not in his machismo culture.

◻ ◻ ◻ ◻ ◻

Things returned to normal fairly quickly. With the danger gone—at least for now—the four of them moved back to Lorenzo's house in Corvallis. Because his shoulder did not hurt or even bleed, Lorenzo ignored the medic's advice to see a doctor.

Sam continued his research, helped by a pretty, young

African-American paralegal in Thad's office. At Lorenzo's suggestion, they borrowed books about Ecuadorian legal procedure through law school libraries at the University of Oregon and Willamette University. Thad's connections assured a swift reply from their emails. The books soon started arriving. "This legal research is right up my alley, so to speak," he said after the first day of working with Vonda.

"Oh yeah, I see that," laughed Lorenzo. "You'll be ready to clerk at the Supreme Court. Just remember to keep your eyes on the law books!"

While the two of them did the research, Lorenzo prepared his opening statement and began to rehearse his arguments based on the legal precedence the students found through their research.

And then there was the matter of Bobbi Bouquet and her trip to Ecuador with him. He set the date for their departure and made business class reservations for the two of them. It would be a long flight that he would much rather make alone, but Bobbi might be key to his defense strategy so he needed to make sure she got there and put on one of the best performances of her career.

He planned to fly to L.A. and arrange to meet her at LAX. He was taking no chances that she would miss the plane.

When things were set, he called Margo Acosta to tell her about the plans for Bobbi's visit. "Hello, *Señora* Acosta, it's Lorenzo Madrid."

"Dear boy, we are much too close for you to be so formal."

"I wanted to tell you that I will be flying to Quito in two days."

"Wonderful news! And will you have a surprise for me?"

"Yes, Margo, Bobbi Bouquet will be with me"

"*Magnifico!* You have made me very happy."

"Are you still planning to put on a movie festival in her honor?"

"Very definitely! I have relied on the tentative date you gave me to make my plans. It seems like that will work. Four days from now—a day after you arrive to allow dear Bobbi time to relax. I have told all of my friends and also the minister of culture. She wants to be involved too. I have allowed her to sponsor Bobbi's visit here. She will secure the films—in Spanish, of course—and pay for the food and drinks. All of Quito's high society will be there, except our *presidente,* who will be on a trade mission to China."

"That is wonderful news, Margo. Thank you so much."

"You must be so proud of your aunt."

"My aunt?"

"Bobbi."

"Yes, I am very proud of her."

"I was thinking we might give others in your country the chance to meet Bobbi."

"What did you have in mind, dear Lorenzo?"

"A visit to the women's prison, Litoral I believe it is called. Bobbi would go and talk to the women and show one of her movies. It would give them a psychological lift."

After a slight hesitation, Margo said, "That is a wonderful idea. Let me talk to the minister herself."

"I think that is all I have to discuss. I can't think of anything else."

"Send me a text about your arrival time and I will take it from there. Chao, my darling. Until we meet again."

When Lorenzo disconnected the phone, he felt a presence at the door of his office. "Who is that big guy at my door?"

Tito giggled. "It is me your only son."

"Son? Son? I did not know I had a son!" Lorenzo extended his arms and the little boy came running, as always leaping into his lap. "I think it is time to go home, Tito. What do you think? And maybe order a pizza."

The boy's face lit up and he jumped down and ran next door to the classroom. "Pizza! Pizza! We are having pizza!" he shouted. "Come on Miss Jo. Get ready for pizza!"

At that moment, Sam walked into the room, his arms loaded with law books. "Whew, boss! If you didn't need glasses before, you'll need them after you get through all these books!"

Lorenzo smiled. "You know, Sam, I'll need a summary of the cases you think pertain. I can't lug all of these tomes to Ecuador."

Sam sighed. "I figured that out so Vonda and I have already started. You'll have them all when you leave. Day after tomorrow?"

"That's right. Enough work for one day. Right now we're all going for pizza."

Sam hesitated and looked embarrassed. "I can't go, boss. Sorry. I have a date."

"With Vonda?"

"Yeah, afraid so."

"Don't worry about it. Go and have a good time."

BECAUSE HE WAS RUNNING OUT OF TIME TO RETURN TO ECUADOR, Lorenzo had to concentrate on reading and absorbing the massive amount of material Sam had gathered for him. As he read the various laws, he highlighted the pertinent parts in yellow and set those pages aside. Sam was assembling these pages and putting them in several binders. Lorenzo also wrote his opening and closing statements. The opening statement read, in part:

> **"Your excellency, I appreciate very much the opportunity to appear before you in this majestic courtroom. I am here in unusual circumstances. I know it is not common practice to allow an attorney from another country to present a case before this court.**
>
> **However, as I think you will agree, this is an unusual case. An American woman, Maxine March, has been accused of kidnapping a minor child and taking him to her country. I will show this court that she did not do this, and that therefore, she did not commit the crime she is accused of committing . . ."**

❑ ❑ ❑ ❑ ❑

"Papa. Are you ever going to love me again?" Tito was standing at the door in his pajamas with tears in his eyes.

"Love you," said Lorenzo, stroking his chin. "Let me think?"

He turned to the boy with his arms outstretched. "Come here." The boy ran to him and jumped into his lap. "Everything I do is for you, Tito. Of course, I love you very much. I am sorry I have been gone so much. I'm trying to make sure you are safe and can stay here forever."

Lorenzo immediately regretted making such a firm statement. How could he know that for certain? The truth was, he couldn't, but he had to act like what he said was true. "I would never let anyone hurt you." He held him close and kissed him on the top of his head. "You know that. Right, pal?"

"Yes, I guess," Tito said, though he looked sad and worried.

"YOU GUESS! NO ONE GUESSES AROUND HERE! NO GUESSES ALLOWED!" Lorenzo got up and swirled the boy around the room until Tito started laughing. "Let's go make chocolate milk. How does that sound?"

"Good, papa."

They walked to the kitchen and Lorenzo heated some milk, filled two cups with spoonfuls of cocoa mix, and stirred up the mixture. For good measure, he got out some cookies Jo had made and put two on a plate next to the cup. "Better?"

"Yes, papa. Better."

"I have to go on another trip, but when I return we will do this all the time."

The boy nodded and finished the snack and said nothing more when Lorenzo carried him into his room and tucked him into bed.

He's been through so much, thought Lorenzo. He avoids things that he doesn't understand.

◻ ◻ ◻ ◻ ◻

Lorenzo didn't go to bed at all. After packing, he took a shower and changed clothes. He waited by the front door for the Uber car and slipped out into the chilly morning when it arrived. He said very little to the driver, a young woman who was probably a college student.

The flight to LAX was on time. As always, it was over-crowded, but Lorenzo was sound asleep even before the plane took off.

He had arranged for Bobbi to meet him at the airport. Doing that necessitated extra expense. She would not come to the airport in a cab or airport shuttle. She had to arrive in a Mercedes limousine, complete with uniformed driver. She could not do a public appearance without bringing many different outfits. Luckily, Lorenzo had talked her out of bringing her own maid. He had sent a message to Margo Acosta asking for help in arranging for an Ecuadorian maid and a car and driver.

Bobbi's usual practice whenever she went out in public was to call old press agent friends for help in tipping off local entertainment reporters that she was going to be in a certain place at a certain time. He'd discouraged her from doing that. "In this case, too much publicity would not be a good thing," he had said.

"I understand," she had whispered. "We'll be on a secret mission!"

So early in the morning at the international terminal, however, preoccupied passengers lost in their newspapers or cell phones and pilots and stewardesses headed for duty walked right by her without noticing. She made a grand entrance anyway.

"Lorenzo, my darling!" she gushed as she led a small army of attendants to the gate. Each was pushing an expensive looking suitcase, all made of matching velvet tapestry.

She was dressed, as the saying goes, to kill. A purple Chanel suit with matching hat. Over that she wore a mink coat, a rarity even in L.A. Lorenzo hoped an environmental activist did not leap out of nowhere and throw red paint on Bobbi and her coat.

When the group reached the gate, Bobbi turned to Lorenzo and whispered, "They'll need generous tips as a reward for taking such good care of me."

The young men lined up in a semi-circle facing Lorenzo. He got five $20 bills from his wallet and gave one to each of them. Bobbi followed him around the circle and kissed each man on both cheeks. "My darlings, you've been lifesavers for me, absolute lifesavers!"

As they bowed and turned to leave, the gate agent yelled, "You can't bring all of these bags onto the plane! They have to be checked. They should have been checked at the front counter! I told you that already, madame!"

Bobbi waved her hand and turned to Lorenzo. "Lorenzo, I know you will take care of this minor unpleasantness, my darling."

Lorenzo walked to the gate agent and quickly made sure each bag was tagged. The gate agent smiled knowingly. "Traveling with elderly relatives can be a real hassle." She winked and helped him with the tagging.

In the meantime, Bobbi had seated herself right on the aisle of the boarding area, assuring, Lorenzo assumed, that she would be seen by all who ventured up to the desk. It didn't take long.

"Aren't you Bonnie Beckett?" said a stout woman in sweatpants and a matching sweat shirt. "I saw you in those movies on Turner Classics—from the 1940s where you played a dumb secretary, I think. My grandmother always loved you. She died last year at 95."

"Oh, I am so sorry for your loss, dear. You're thinking of Ann Sothern as 'Maisie.' She was a star long before I was even born."

"Okay, if you say so," said the woman as she lumbered off unconvinced and shaking her head.

Lorenzo sat down next to Bobbi who put on a brave face.

"Didn't you used to be somebody?" said a voice.

Luckily, the plane was called before Bobbi had to answer.

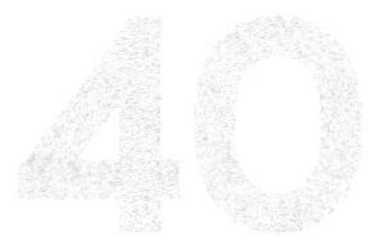

LUCKILY FOR LORENZO, the handsome and smooth steward Alex was on duty in business class for their flight. Lorenzo pulled him aside as another steward was escorting Bobbi to her seat. "This woman, Bobbi Bouquet, is an actress," he explained. "She used to be an important actress, but does not get very many roles now. She does not know her star has dimmed, so-to-speak. I am escorting her to Ecuador to appear at a festival of her movies. She still has a lot of fans in Latin America. It would help me a lot if you could keep her occupied as much as you have time for. I know you have many other duties so I will understand if you can't do this."

"Lorenzo, my darling," Bobbi yelled from her seat. "Where is my wonderful Lorenzo?"

Alex smiled knowingly. "I am used to dealing with rich, older women. I will do my best for you."

Lorenzo walked forward to his seat. "Are you comfortable, Bobbi?"

"Yes, of course, but I would be more comfortable if you were next to me so I could hold your hand in rough weather."

"Yes, of course," said Lorenzo with a sheepish grin.

"A mimosa, Madame Bouquet?" Alex was saving Lorenzo already.

"Oh, how divine. Thank you . . ."

"Alejandro Panza, madame, at your service. My friends call me Alex."

"And I know I will want to be your friend, Alex," said Bobbi, her eyelids fluttering.

Alex placed the drink on the console between them. "*Señor?*"

"Yes, please," said Lorenzo.

"A light brunch will be served as soon as we are airborne."

Lorenzo raised his glass in a toast to Bobbi.

"This is all so marvelous," said Bobbi, draining the glass in one gulp. "And I owe it all to you, my darling." Another steward filled her glass immediately. "Now you must tell me what I must do to fulfill my end of our bargain."

For the next fifteen minutes, Lorenzo brought Bobbi up to date on his work for Maxine.

"Poor darling," she said after drinking her third mimosa. "And how is the boy?"

"He is worried about my being absent, but otherwise fine."

Lorenzo could not admit to her that he wished he could adopt Tito himself. This wish contradicted his oath as a lawyer to help his clients any way he could. Did he really want to win this case? He pushed the answer aside for now.

"What do you want me to do, my darling?"

Lorenzo handed Bobbi a blue folder. "I have prepared a outline which details your role in this project. It gives you background to the case and the scenario of how I hope it turns out."

Bobbi took the folder but did not open it. "Can you give me a synopsis? I'm a quick learner but I like to know in advance what I'm learning."

They looked up to find Alex and the other steward, Rodrigo, standing with trays of food. "Your brunch, *Señora* Bouquet and *Señor* Madrid."

"*Muchas gracias, Alejandro y Rodrigo,*" said Lorenzo.

"I love the sound of Spanish words," said Bobbi. "So romantic, so thrilling. I recall a love scene I once had with Ricardo Montalbán—a very dashing actor and a good kisser. He was also very handsome like all three of you. I remember . . ." She glanced at the tray. "Quiche and crepes both! How grand!" She quickly tackled her breakfast. "Marvelous!" she said with her mouth full. The two stewards departed.

Finished, Bobbi pushed the tray away, put on glasses with rhinestone covered frames and opened the folder. "So let's see what I must do to fill this role."

As Lorenzo had guessed, Bobbi would be most comfortable treating all of this as a movie role. "In our little story, you are a movie queen who is appearing at a film festival before fans who love you," said Lorenzo.

"I love the sound of that: movie queen. Maybe we'll see if I am as big as I've heard in a foreign country."

She frowned and looked sad. "They've forgotten me at home. But what do they know, right my darling?"

"Yes, right," said Lorenzo, his mouth full of a bagel. He glanced around and lowered his voice. "The person we are trying to impress is the woman who invited you here, Margo Acosta. Very wealthy and very well-connected. She knows a lot of people in government from the president on down. Her late husband was a diplomat for years. She is the reason my client is in prison."

Bobbi looked shocked. "Then why are we dealing with her at all?"

"I'm going to turn her and you're going to help me."

"I love a challenge," said Bobbi, her eyes sparkling. "But how? Is she lesbian? I played one in my film *Canal Street Girl*. Of course we could only hint at that kind of thing in those days. But I could try to do it."

"No, I don't think she'd be interested. She loves you as the star she never was. She will be reflected in your glory these next few days. I want you to kill her with kindness, so to speak. I want you to suggest to her that Maxine needs to be released for humanitarian reasons and deported. She is sick after being in a really horrible prison for a month. I think she has TB."

"Poor dear."

"As I was saying, spend time with Margo. Tell her stories about Hollywood. Talk about that movie you were both in."

"Ah yes, *The Bride Wore Blood.* She was only an extra, as I recall. I don't remember her at all, to tell you the truth, my darling. I don't remember much about the movie either. I was making three or four a year in those days."

"This will be where your acting skills come in, plus a little bit of lying."

"I can do that," said Bobbi. "I've done a good share of that in my time. A girl has to do what a girl has to do."

Lorenzo continued to go over the scenario with Bobbi. She becomes Margo's good friend and does the film festival. She meets with whomever Margo wants her to meet. She is wined and dined by only the best people in Ecuadorian society. She hints at her involvement in future movie projects in Ecuador. All of this to buy time."

"And what, pray tell, is this all leading to?"

"It all depends on the outcome of my case. While you are doing all of this 'courting,' I am hard at work defending Maxine *in* court. If she is found innocent and set free, we all fly home together."

"And if she is found guilty?"

"Let's just say at this point that the end game will have you taking your films to the prison."

"And?" said Bobbi.

"I'm still working on that."

"Delicious! I love cliffhangers!

41

TRUE TO HER WORD, Margo Acosta had arranged for a special welcome for Bobbi. Alex came to their seats about an hour before landing in Quito. "*Señora* Bouquet." Bobbi was dozing but her eyes opened when she heard his voice.

"*Señor* Lorenzo." He touched Lorenzo's arm.

"I wanted to inform you that we have had word from the airport that a large delegation is waiting for you."

"What kind of delegation?"

"A lot of people with signs of welcome."

"Margo came through," Lorenzo muttered. He turned to Bobbi who had not yet registered the news.

"Your public, Bobbi. They are at the airport waiting for you."

"How wonderful. I must get ready for them."

She got out of her seat and fished a large bag out of the overhead bin. She walked down the aisle towards the lavatory, stopping to confer with Alex along the way. She disappeared into the tiny lavatory. A female steward who had been working the other side of the business section followed her inside.

Lorenzo gathered up the various papers he had consulted for his briefing of Bobbi. He glanced over his opening statement one more time.

"There now, this is a much better look, don't you think my darling?" said Bobbi a half hour later.

Lorenzo looked up to see a person transformed—Bobbi wearing a gold lamé gown with a shawl that had pearls sewn into it. Her makeup was flawless and made her look years younger. Her hair, pulled back into a bun, was covered with a lace mantilla. Bobbi the attractive older woman was now Bobbi the movie star. She seemed to float down the aisle towards him.

"You look amazing!" he said, kissing her outstretched hand. "You are a star again!"

"What do you mean, 'again'? I have been a star since before you were born, my darling."

"Yes, of course," he said.

After the plane had landed, two stewards barred the door to the tourist section so Bobbi and Lorenzo could get off first.

"Thanks, Alex. I couldn't have done this without you." He pressed a $50 bill into Alex's hand.

Bobbi hugged him and Alejandro and stopped in the doorway.

"Okay, are you ready?" asked Lorenzo. Ahead was a virtual sea of official looking people on the tarmac crowding around the stairway.

"I'm ready for my close up, Mr. DeMille," she laughed.

Lorenzo hung back out of sight to allow her to bask in the momentary glory. For all her excesses, he had to admit that Bobbi was still a star in the old Hollywood way.

As she started down the stairway, the crowd started to applaud. Then, from behind a chain link fence at the edge of the asphalt, came loud cheers and whistles and clapping. Margo was standing at the foot of the stairs next to an elderly man in a tuxedo and sporting the obligatory sash that all Latin American officials seem to favor.

When Bobbi reached the ground, two young girls rushed up and handed her bouquets of flowers. She hugged both girls. Margo came next, kissing her on both cheeks in that time-honored continental way. Next, the older gentleman clicked his heels together and bowed, before doing a kind of air kiss. (Perhaps his wife was watching.) He handed Bobbi what might have been a key to the city, which she did not know where to put. Margo handed it to her chauffeur.

Then there was a band playing "Stars and Stripes Forever," a little out-of-tune. Margo was leaving nothing to chance.

Lorenzo started down the stairs followed by the other now very impatient business class passengers. When he reached the ground, Alberto materialized out of nowhere.

"God, am I glad to see you!" he said, hugging him tightly. "This is a real circus! Where's the car? Hey, I like your beard!"

Alberto rubbed his face and smiled. "I needed to look older," he shrugged. He pointed to an embassy car with a driver behind the wheel parked near the diplomatic gate they had driven in and out of before.

"Give me a minute and come with me. I may have other plans for you." Lorenzo walked over to Bobbi, Margo, and the older official as they were beginning to walk toward Margo's waiting limousine.

"Oh, there's my darling Lorenzo," said Bobbi, linking her arm in his.

Margo walked over to him, kissed him on both cheeks, and introduced him to the *señor,* one of the vice-mayors of Quito, who shook his hand.

"What are your plans, *Señora* Acosta?" Lorenzo asked.

"I would like your aunt to be my guest at my home here in Quito. You are welcome to stay there as well."

"Thank you, but no. I have to prepare for Maxine March's court appearance, which is scheduled for the day after tomorrow."

He turned to Alberto. "This is my assistant/body guard here in Ecuador, Alberto Dragón. I want him to be with you at all times during your visit."

If Alberto was surprised at his new responsibility, he didn't show it.

"Another handsome Latin man," gushed Bobbi. "And I love

the beard. It is very sexy!"

Alberto bowed and touched his face. *"Mucho gusto, señora."*

"I absolutely love this, Lorenzo," said Bobbi. "I know I will be safe in Alberto's strong hands. And I like the part about him being with me at all times." She winked at Lorenzo.

Alberto blushed and moved forward, taking Bobbi by the arm and guiding her to Margo's limousine.

"What is the plan for today?" asked Lorenzo.

"I will take dear Bobbi to my home to rest," said Margo. "I have a group of friends coming to dinner. Tomorrow afternoon is the film festival followed by a reception at the Ministry of Culture. You must come to both of them."

"I will certainly be there. One more thing before we part. Did you have any success in setting up some kind of event for Bobbi at the prison? We mentioned it in passing when I was here before."

Bobbi turned away from the crowd, still applauding and whistling, to join their conversation.

"I am still trying. Security is very tight now because of all these tiresome terrorists. An old beau of mine is in charge of all the prisons in my country so it could still happen."

"That would mean a lot to me," said Bobbi. "I mean, bringing a bit of glamour to those poor unfortunate women, locked up without a key!"

Margo's eyes flashed momentarily. "I can assure you, dear Bobbi, that they all got a fair trial."

Bobbi ignored her. "I was in prison once," she said, proudly. "We filmed some of *San Quentin Undercover* in that wretched place. I played a reporter pretending to be . . ."

"Let me help you get into the car," said Margo. Alberto slid into the front seat and they departed, the crowds still cheering and the off-key band still playing "Stars and Stripes Forever" over and over again.

42

LORENZO MET WITH KURT JENKINS as soon as he got to the embassy. He filled him in on what he planned to do if Maxine was convicted.

"I don't want to know the specifics," he said. "I figured you had a reason for bringing the actress back with you."

"She's a diversion, pure and simple. She is our ticket into the prison."

"So you think you'll lose."

"I can't see how we won't. The evidence is very strong. She has the boy. He was taken out of this country, but not by her. That might help but it would mean shifting the blame to Paul Bickford. He actually took the boy away. But how do I prove it without him here to admit it under oath and risk arrest himself?"

"That's a problem," said Jenkins, "and we don't know where he is."

"I'll get Bobbi there to put on her show and then I'll improvise. I don't think you should go anywhere near any of this. You've done enough."

"So far, I haven't done anything I wouldn't do for any U.S. citizen in peril."

"Believe me, you've gone way beyond simple help. One thing, though, I would like to continue to use Alberto. He's very resourceful and, I think, brave, not to mention young and strong. I will need him for the next two days."

"No problem at all," said Jenkins.

"One thing I should tell you, if things get really bad and you have to leave Ecuador unexpectedly, Alberto has dual citizenship."

"Thanks for telling me. Good to know."

Jenkins stood up. "I'll leave you to your preparations. I'll see you at the movie festival tomorrow."

With his legal briefs ready and his opening and closing statements ready, Lorenzo created a chart of what would be happening: movie festival, appearance at the prison, and . . . The trill of his phone interrupted his thoughts. "Hello."

"Boss, it's Alberto."

"Yes, Berto, how's it going?"

"Okay, I guess."

"You **guess**! Is something wrong?

"Kinda. Between Bobbi and this Margo chick, they've got the hots for me! I'm not kidding. They both came on to me after dinner. In the hall outside Bobbi's room, in that gallery room with all the photos of actresses and such."

"What did you do?"

"I got the hell out of there! I told them something had come up and you needed me back at the embassy."

"Good thinking. You on your way back here?"

"No boss, I'm at the front gate now!"

43

A LOUD KNOCK RESOUNDED THROUGHOUT LORENZO'S ROOM. He opened the door and Alberto hustled inside. "Close the door! I wouldn't put it past those ladies to stalk me even in the embassy! Do you have anything to drink?"

"Sit down, Berto. You need to calm down and breathe."

He crossed the room and poured brandy for both of them. He sat down opposite Alberto. "Tell me what happened."

"Those old gals are hornier than hell," he said, a look of fear in his eyes. "They almost jumped me. After dinner when I said I was tired and wanted to go to bed early. That Margo woman said she would take me to the room where you stayed. Not sure where her secretary was but she wasn't anywhere that I saw. So she leads me there by the hand and your friend, the actress followed."

Lorenzo held his hand over his mouth to hide his smile. "What did you do?"

"I pretended that my cell phone was ringing and told them you needed me back here right then. That worked and they both looked sad. Your friend, the actress . . ."

"Bobbi."

"Yeah, Bobbi." She said she liked brown-skinned men like me. *Dios mío!* She's old enough to be my mother or even my grandmother!"

"She used that line on me too," Lorenzo said with a grimace.

"Lorenzo, you didn't . . "

"God, no!"

"Then the rich lady . . . Margo. She said she'd had sex with more brown-skinned men than Bobbi."

"Sounds like you dodged a bullet," said Lorenzo.

"I'd have needed a bullet if I woke up next to one of them!"

Lorenzo could not hold back his laughter any longer. He started giggling and that turned into laughter so forceful that his eyes started to water.

"Better me than you, I guess. Right boss?"

"Oh yes. Our whole case revolves around the good will of these two lades. You did well. Thank you."

After Alberto calmed down and went to his room, Lorenzo called Bobbi on her cell phone. Given her insomnia, he knew she'd be awake.

"Lorenzo, my darling," she said. "So good to hear your wonderful voice. We missed you tonight. And your handsome assistant had to go too. Important business at the embassy, I guess."

"Yes, I needed his help to prepare my case. Are you settled in?"

"Yes, very much so. Margo Acosta is a wonderful hostess. She has provided me with a maid and expensive lingerie and a fortune in cosmetics. My suite is very luxurious."

"Did you see her shrine to you, I mean the room with all the photos of you?

"I did and I loved it. Seeing the **me** from long ago . . . Well I guess not **that** long ago. It got me feeling young again and wishing I could start over. I was a star you know." She sniffled.

"You still are a star, Bobbi," said Lorenzo. "I mean it! Doing this for me has taken courage and no small amount of acting."

"Thank you, my darling. Now tell me what you want me to do tomorrow."

"Just be yourself and let the evening happen. You and I will get through this together."

44

MARGO ACOSTA INSISTED ON USING HER MERCEDES LIMOUSINE, complete with chauffeur, for Bobbi's ride to the Ministry of Culture building. Bobbi and Margo were just emerging as Lorenzo and Alberto drove up in a taxi. Margo's servants, lined up on both sides of the front steps, started applauding as the two ladies appeared in the doorway. At first, it didn't seem like Margo would yield the spotlight to Bobbi. After the actress glared at her and mumbled something under her breath, she stepped back.

"*GRACIAS, MI AMIGOS,*" she shouted, as she walked slowly down the steps to the car. "You are very kind."

Lorenzo stepped forward and took Bobbi by the arm. "Who are these two beautiful ladies?" he said. "I am very lucky tonight."

"I might say the same for the two of you," she said. "Tuxedos make the man."

Both smiled and got into the car. Lorenzo followed and sat on the jump seat and Alberto took the seat next to the driver. As the car drove through the gates of Margo's villa, two motorcycles took position up ahead.

"Margo, you have left nothing to chance," said Lorenzo. "This is such a nice tribute to Bobbi."

"Much deserved, believe me."

Bobbi nodded and began waving to passersby on the street. Although he doubted they were there to see her, Lorenzo knew that Bobbi wouldn't care.

People were people and she thought anyone can be made into a fan with a little effort.

As the car pulled up to the ministry building, the same band that had been at the airport struck up "Stars and Stripes Forever." As they emerged to loud applause from the formally dressed people lining the red-carpeted steps, the band began to play other music that Lorenzo was not familiar with.

"My God," exclaimed Bobbi, "those are selections from the soundtracks of several of my films. Let me think, *Dodge City Girl, Moscow Undercover,* and *The Rapes of Graft.*"

She turned to Margo. "You outdid yourself, my dear. How can I ever repay you?"

"It was my pleasure, Bobbi. You might do one thing to make me very happy."

"Yes, yes. Anything!"

"In your remarks, you might mention that we first met in Hollywood when we played opposite one another in *The Bride Wore Blood.*"

Lorenzo wondered how Bobbi would react to this bit of wishful thinking on Margo's part. She had been a lowly extra who Bobbi did not remember on that movie. He hoped for all their sakes that she came up with a good answer.

"Of course, my dear Margo," she cooed. "I will talk about your acting ability at such a young age and in a language not your native language."

Margo beamed as another sash-wearing official greeted them with kisses on the hand and both cheeks.

"*Señora* Bobbi Bouquet," said Margo, "may I present Humberto Diaz de Santa Clara, vice-minister of culture. The minister was called away."

"Your name suits you, *señora.* A flower in every sense of that word. Please follow me into the auditorium for your remarks and then a showing of some of your films."

Bobbi, Margo, Lorenzo, Alberto, and the minister walked through the large foyer and into a large auditorium. As the crowd saw them, they burst into loud applause. When Bobbi wobbled a bit, Lorenzo steadied her and handed her a handkerchief. "They love you, Bobbi. Take it slowly. I'm here beside you."

The vice-minister led Bobbi onto the stage and Margo, Lorenzo, and Alberto sat in seats in the first row. The applause died down when the vice-minister stepped to the microphone.

"*Señoras y caballeros. Bienvenido.*" He reviewed Bobbi's career and mentioned her continued popularity in Latin America. He noted the role that Margo Acosta had played in bringing her to Quito for the festival.

When Bobbi stepped to the podium she looked, to Lorenzo, every inch a star. The gown, the jewelry, the hair, and perfect makeup brought to mind a Hollywood that one seldom saw any more. "I am overcome with emotion," she began, with a translator repeating her words. "You have made me very happy, really happy beyond words. Thank you from the bottom of my heart." More applause. "It is a special pleasure to be in this beautiful theater with all of you splendid ladies and gentlemen, my friends from the U.S. who are here with me, and especially my old friend from early in her career and mine, Margo Acosta. Margo."

Margo walked onto the stage and bowed, and then she kissed Bobbi on both cheeks.

Not a good idea to outshine the star, Margo, thought Lorenzo. Take your seat. Margo seemed about to speak into the micro-phone, but Bobbi quickly shook her hand and turned her around and aimed her towards her own seat in a deft move that Margo probably did not notice.

"We played together in the horror film, *The Bride Wore Blood*. It is a wonderful example of a genre that has retained its popular-ity. I could tell then that Margo had real star potential. It was a loss to the world of cinema when she got married and left us for the exciting world of government and diplomacy."

I told you to praise Margo, thought Lorenzo, but you are laying it on a big too thick. Thunderous applause broke his train of thought and Margo stood up again until Bobbi reclaimed the microphone. "As we say in Hollywood, on with the show!" said Bobbi in a loud voice.

As he had been several years before, Lorenzo was surprised both by Bobbi's acting ability and the durability of the films. Except for some of the production values, most could be made successfully today. After the movie excerpts ended, Bobbi and Margo walked from the auditorium into an ornate ballroom, which was filled with the well-dressed people from the festival, tables of food, and waiters strolling around with trays of champagne in crystal glasses.

When he could get away from the ladies, Lorenzo walked over to Kurt Jenkins. "Glad you came," he said. "It's a real zoo."

"I've never been sure why you brought the actress down here," said Jenkins.

"Purely as a distraction for Margo Acosta. When I found out she was such a big Bobbi Bouquet fan, I lied and told her Bobbi was my aunt."

Jenkins shook his head. "What difference will that make?"

"Damned if I know," said Lorenzo. "My thought was that with her many connections to government officials, Margo might be able to influence them to go easy on Maxine."

"Wrong thought, I fear," said Jenkins. "This is a kidnapping case! Whatever the circumstances are with this little boy, that is the proverbial bottom line."

"I know you're right, Kurt," said Lorenzo, shaking his head. "But I had to try something—for everyone's sake."

"If you lose—I should say **when** you lose—you need a fallback plan." Jenkins handed him a folded piece of paper. "This may help if it comes to that. But you didn't get this from me. In fact, I'm going on home leave for a month starting tomorrow. For the sake of my career, I need what we call 'plausible deniability.' It was a pleasure to meet you. I wish you good luck."

"Kurt, you have gone way beyond your duty to help American citizens in trouble. Thank you. I hope we meet again."

As Jenkins walked out of the room, Lorenzo unfolded the paper.

Desperate times call for desperate measures.
If Maxine loses her case, be at the side entrance
of the courthouse tomorrow at one. Your man,
Alberto, will be waiting in a dark blue sedan.
Bring Maxine and the actress.
P.B.

AT TEN THE NEXT MORNING, an embassy car picked up Lorenzo and drove him to the Acosta mansion. Lorenzo had told Bobbi to be packed, but pack light, because they wouldn't be returning to the house. Margo walked out with Bobbi. "I can't tell you what a pleasure it has been to host you," she said, giving her the obligatory peck on both cheeks. "You'll be in touch about those movie projects?"

"Indeed, I will," smiled Bobbi.

"Will you be at the court?" asked Margo.

"Oh yes, I want to see my nephew in action."

Lorenzo felt a knot in his stomach at this lie. "Are you going to be there too?" he asked, knowing that Margo was the one who started all of this by turning Maxine in to the police.

"Oh yes, I will be there in the front row. I, too, want to see the great Lorenzo Madrid in action!"

¤ ¤ ¤ ¤ ¤

The three of them, joined by Alberto Dragón, walked through the metal detector and up the stairs to the court-room. Fortunately, the demonstrators had been kept away.

"I'll see you later," Lorenzo said to the other three. I need to go into this door.

As before, Sebastión Blanco, the

court administrator, met him inside. *"Buenos días, señor. Señorita* March has been driven to the court."

"Buenos días, Señor Blanco. Thank you for telling me."

"Come right this way."

Lorenzo sat down at the defense table as the only attorney. The local co-counsel the embassy had promised hadn't contacted him. He felt comfortable doing this alone, however. Laura Nieto the translator was there, and that was a comfort to Lorenzo because of his rusty Spanish.

There was a commotion at the doorway as photographers jostled for position. Bobbi walked in as cameras clicked and flashbulbs flashed.

After the court audience had assembled, the doors were closed. All heads turned to the right as the door to the cells opened and Maxine March walked in.

She looked worse than before. Even dressed in the so-called "better" street clothes that Dawn had found for her, her clothes hung on her thin frame. Her makeup had been hastily applied so that she looked like a ghost.

Lorenzo got up and walked to her side, holding on to her arm and guiding her to the chair next to him. "How are you holding up," he whispered.

"Not so good. Dawn tried to fix me up but it's too late. I know I'm a mess. I'd hate to have Tito see me like this."

Guilt washed over Lorenzo like a wave in a rough ocean. How could he ever think that Tito was his little boy when this woman had gone through so much to protect him?

"He wouldn't care as long as he could be with you," said Lorenzo. "We'll get through this. It'll be tough, but we'll get through this together— for Tito!"

Lorenzo turned and nodded to Bobbi and Margo sitting together two rows back.

"Don't look around now, but there are two older women sitting a few rows back. One is the woman who turned you in, Margo

Acosta. Pay no attention to her. The other is a movie actress named Bobbi Bouquet. She is a friend. Go along with whatever she says. She is your only character witness, even though you don't know her. The world thinks she's my aunt. We'll be improvising but it'll help. Okay?"

"I guess." Maxine's face looked blank and Lorenzo doubted she understood what he had said. At that moment, he wished they'd allowed him to bring Bobbi to meet Maxine. Too late for that now.

The court proceeding began. With everyone standing, the large carved door to the rear of the bench opened and the judge walked in. He was the same judge who had presided before, Jorge Ponte, a senior judge, presumably with a lot of experience. He also spoke excellent English. He had allowed Maxine to be moved to the clinic in the courthouse and ordered better food for her. Those were humane gestures.

In Spanish and English, Blanco announced the convening of the court. The judge began by reciting again the charges against Maxine. "In her appearance before this court two weeks ago, the defendant, *Señorita* Maxine March, was charged with the crime of kidnapping a minor child of Ecuadorian citizenship."

Lorenzo stood up. "May I speak, your excellency?"

The judge gestured for him to sit down. "You will have time to object, *Señor* Madrid, but that time is not now! Sit down!"

In Spanish, the judge read once again a summary of the case, with Laura whispering the translation to Lorenzo.

He turned to Lorenzo and Maxine. "I must caution you not to interrupt this court at inappropriate times. I think the same rule is followed in court in the United States. Am I not correct in this assumption?"

"Yes, your excellency. It won't happen again."

What followed was the presentation of the case by a state prosecutor, a woman in her forties, unsmiling and very well-prepared. She began calling witnesses, whose depositions had been presented at the earlier hearing.

There was the official Maxine had talked to at the immigration ministry. ("She said she was working on behalf of friends who wanted to adopt a child. In fact, she was asking me questions that pertained to herself, and she already had taken the boy to the U.S.!")

"Objection!"

"Overruled."

The clerk from the hotel in Montecristi. ("She was showing me a photo of a young boy and asking if I knew who he was. I did not know.")

The policeman who found her in an abandoned house. ("It looked strange to have her poking around in this ruined house. I thought she was a thief. I think she took some papers out of a trunk.")

Father Castillo, who directed her to where the boy's family might still live. ("She seemed nervous and fretful. I offered her a cup of tea, but she refused. At the time I did not know if she ever found the house or any details about the boy. I did not see her again.")

Lorenzo had no way to deny anything these people had said and it really made no difference. Maxine had been there and asked about the boy. This evidence showed what the law calls "intent."

"The state calls *Señora* Margo Acosta." Margo did not look at either Lorenzo or Maxine on her way to the witness box where she was sworn in.

"Please tell the court how you came to know the defendant."

"I met her in front of the house which the policeman caught her robbing."

"Objection! My client was looking for documentation to aid her adoption request. One can hardly rob a shack! Was there a buried treasure in there?"

"I caution you not to try the patience of this court," said the judge. "Kidnapping is a serious crime that we in this country do not take lightly!"

"I am sorry, your excellency. I did not mean to appear to be making fun of this case or the serious issue it has come to signify. I am very sorry."

"Proceed, madam prosecutor."

"What happened next, *señora?*"

"I invited her to come to my house for tea. I do admit, though, that I was curious as to why an American woman would be prowling around the back streets of Montecristi . . ."

"Objection! My client was not 'prowling' anywhere. She was looking for documentation about the boy's past."

"A boy she had already kidnapped!" snapped Margo.

"Objection sustained. Please confine your remarks to the actual events of that day. Proceed." Lorenzo smiled at this tiny victory.

"At my home, she told me about the real purpose of her trip to Ecuador."

"And that was what?"

"To build a case for keeping the boy, I presume. A boy she had already kidnapped!"

"Objection!"

"Overruled. Anything else, *Señora* Acosta?"

"*Eso es todo, su excelencia.*" (That is all, your excellency.)

"The prosecution rests, *su excelencia,*" said the prosecutor.

"*Señor* Madrid."

"*Muchas gracias, su excelencia.*"

"May I ask some questions of *Señora* Acosta, while she is on the stand?"

"Yes," said the judge. "Proceed."

"Good afternoon, *Señora* Acosta. We have met before, several times."

"*Sí, señor.*"

"Is it not true that you befriended me, both in Quito and

Montecristi in order to get information to use against my client in this trial."

"Objection," shouted the prosecutor.

"WHY DO YOU HATE MY CLIENT SO MUCH?" shouted Lorenzo to be heard over the judge's ruling.

"*Señor* Madrid, one more outburst like that and I will have you removed from my court and put in jail. You will not like our jails here, believe me."

"I am very sorry, *su excelencia*. I hold no bad feelings towards you or this court, believe me. It is just hard to control my anger when I hear such lies!"

He turned to Margo. "That is all I have to ask you."

Margo's eyes flashed as she walked by Lorenzo. "You will regret this," she hissed. "Bobbi's appearance at the prison is cancelled!"

As if that really mattered, thought Lorenzo.

"I will not have you darken my nephew's reputation in this way," said a voice from the audience. "You are a Jezebel!"

Bobbi Bouquet stood up and rushed towards the departing Margo. When they met in the aisle, Bobbi hit Margo so hard in the jaw that she fell to her knees.

Guards rushed in, both to restrain Bobbi and to help Margo walk from the courtroom. She left rubbing her jaw.

"WHO IS THIS WOMAN?" shouted the judge.

"She is my aunt," said Lorenzo, a sheepish look on his face. "She came with me to act as a character witness for my client, who she has known for many years."

By this time, Bobbi had walked to the defense table and sat down, a look of victory on her face.

The judge said nothing for several minutes. Lorenzo braced for the worst: he and Bobbi would be held in contempt and thrown in jail.

"*Señora* Bouquet . . . Like an arrangement of flowers?"

"Yes sir."

"You were a big movie star. My wife has seen all of your pictures. She will be thrilled that I met you."

"Actually, sir, I am still a big movie star," said Bobbi. "And I will be happy to write something special for her. More than just an autograph."

"*Muchas gracias, señora.*"

He looked at Lorenzo, who was bewildered by what was happening in front of him. You may proceed, *Señor* Madrid."

"The defense calls Maxine March."

Maxine got to her feet haltingly and Lorenzo walked over to her and helped her to the witness box. He had debated calling her at all, but decided he had no other option. Things were not looking all that good. The chance for an acquittal or her release were growing slimmer by the minute.

After she had been sworn in by the clerk, Lorenzo began. "Good afternoon, Miss March. I hope you are feeling better today."

Maxine shrugged her shoulders and then began to cough.

"Could we have water, please?"

The clerk filled a glass and carried it to Maxine. She gulped it down quickly. The clerk refilled the glass. The judge motioned for her to leave the pitcher on the witness stand.

"Please tell us the circumstances of your coming to Ecuador several years ago."

Maxine, on assignment in Ecuador, told the story of needing to get away from men who were after her because of the illegal activity she had seen in the jungle with her friend, a French photographer. Several American Special Operations officers helped her get away after her friend was killed. One of the men took her to Montecristi to keep her safe until her rescue.

"I must interrupt, *su excelencia,*" said Lorenzo. "May I approach the bench?"

The judge nodded. Lorenzo handed him a folder. "This is an order from the United States Government preventing me from naming these two men at this time. Their names—and their work—are classified. I don't think names matter in this case any-way. These documents also indicate that they were operating in Ecuador at that time."

The judge read the papers and nodded.

"You may proceed, *señor.*"

"Please go on, *Señorita* March."

"As the men were closing in on me, someone I had known for some time arrived with a squad of his own men. There was a gun battle and my friend got me out of there."

"Objection!" said the prosecutor. "This sounds like a fantasy novel or a Mexican telenovella. It is hard to believe any of it."

At this point, Maxine started to cry so her answer came out indistinctly. "It is all true!" She also started coughing again.

Lorenzo stood up and shouted. "THE PROSECUTOR IS BADGERING THIS WITNESS!"

"Sit down, *señor,*" said the judge. He turned to the prosecutor. "You will have ample time to cross-examine the witness. Please continue, *Señorita* March."

Maxine dried her eyes. "As we were lifting off . . .."

"Lifting off?" interrupted the judge.

"In a helicopter. My friend and his men had flown to Montecristi in a helicopter."

"Must have been considered an important mission to send a helicopter for you," said the judge. "Do you work for the United States Government?"

"No sir, I do not. My friend did all this for me. We have been close for a long time."

"That must be an understatement," said the judge, shaking his head. "But I do not see how the boy fits into all of this."

"Tito had lived in Montecristi all his life and my friend had met him on previous trips there. He loved Americans and wanted to act as their guide around the village. If they wanted to buy Panama hats or find a good restaurant, he would help them. Their tips helped him survive. He was an orphan, as I guess you already know. He befriended me in the same way."

"Please take us back to the night you were rescued by your friend," said Lorenzo.

Maxine coughed into her handkerchief again.

"My friend arrived with his men, battled the drug guys who were after me, and we ran to the helicopter. As we were lifting off, we looked down on a heart-wrenching scene. The boy, Tito, had flung himself on the ground and was sobbing uncontrollably."

At this point, Maxine broke down, her body shaking with constant coughing.

"*Su excelencia,*" said Lorenzo. "May we have a recess?"

"*Absoluto!*"

❑ ❑ ❑ ❑ ❑

The judge allowed Lorenzo to go with Maxine to the holding cell. Bobbi tagged along, surprising Lorenzo with her compassion towards someone other than herself. "Give me something soft, like a rag or your handkerchief," she said. She dosed it with water from a bottle and dabbed at Maxine's face. "Lie down on this bench and take deep breaths. I'm not sure this will help but I did it in one of my movies, *Valiant Nurse* or *Battlefield Angel*. I can't remember the title but I remember that I played a brave nurse."

She turned to Lorenzo who was standing next to her, looking worried. "She's in bad shape, but I guess you know that," she whispered. "She needs to go to a hospital now."

"I know that, but it just isn't possible," he said, shaking his head. "I need to cut this short and end this charade of a trial. The authorities think she's guilty and nothing I can say in the courtroom will change the verdict. Maybe we can appeal it, but I doubt she'd make it between now and a retrial."

Blanco, the court administrator, appeared in the doorway.

"We need to resume the trial," he said, looking at his watch impatiently. "There are other cases to be heard. This is but one of many."

Lorenzo and Bobbi helped Maxine sit up. Bobbi rummaged in her giant purse and came up with a hairbrush, lipstick, and a compact. She brushed Maxine's hair and applied both lipstick and makeup quickly and, to Lorenzo's unpracticed eye, expertly.

"There, my dear, you look much better," said Bobbi, stepping back to scrutinize her work.

She and Lorenzo helped Maxine to her feet and led her back to the courtroom. As he pulled out a chair, Lorenzo glanced at the audience. In the middle of the attorneys and curious townspeople from before the break, a new person sat two rows back.

Staff Sergeant James Porten, his Special Ops jungle rescuer, was dressed in a suit and wearing a tie. He had even cut his hair. He nodded once in acknowledgement. Lorenzo nodded back. In his heart, he knew things might be changing for the better—and soon.

46

WHEN THEY RESUMED, the judge seemed to be wrapping things up. Lorenzo had expected a chance for rebuttal of the prosecutor's charges and the testimony of the witnesses.

"*Su excelencia*, I did not think that the trial would be ending so quickly. I have not had a chance to comment on what the witnesses said. Especially, I want to rebut the testimony of *Señora* Acosta. What she said simply was not true. And she was definitely prejudiced against my client long before she came into this court. I would hope you would call her back to allow me this opportunity."

The judge waved his hand as if ridding himself of Lorenzo's remarks. "I fear that time has passed, Mr. Madrid. Let me read you once again the statute in Ecuadorian law that must govern this case. He put on his glasses and opened the book in front of him. "Ecuador is party to the Hague Convention on Protection of Children and Cooperation in Respect of Intercountry Adoption. Pursuant to those requirements . . ."

Lorenzo stopped listening because he knew the statute by heart. If that was the law governing this case—with no consideration of circumstances like Tito being an orphan— Maxine was doomed.

" . . . Therefore, prospective parents must obtain a full and final adoption under Ecuadorian law before the child can emigrate to the United States."

The judge removed his glasses. "As

we all know, none of this happened. Your client lied about all aspects of this case from the moment she arrived in Ecuador a month or so ago. She claims not to know how the boy got to the United States. But we have proof that he is there. The photo of the two of them standing in front of a sign in Oregon proves that. Although we do not know how he got there—and perhaps she does not know either—the fact remains that he is there and she is caring for him. The sentiment is laudable but what she did is unlawful." He stood up.

"Please rise," intoned Blanco.

Maxine got to her feet, supported on one side by Lorenzo and the other by Laura, the translator.

"*Señorita* Maxine March, I find you guilty of kidnapping a minor child, a citizen of Ecuador, and sentence you to a term of ten years in prison."

At that point, Maxine slumped into Lorenzo's arms. Bobbi rushed up, pushing away the guards who tried to stop her. She dabbed water on Maxine's face and supported her head so she could drink without choking. She and Lorenzo helped her stand up and supported her as she stumbled toward the door to the holding cell.

"NOOOOOOOOOOO!" Her cry was like that of a wounded animal. Lorenzo knew that he would never forget it.

47

BOBBI WAS ALLOWED TO STAY WITH MAXINE IN THE HOLDING CELL while arrangements were made to transport her back to the prison in Guayaquil. Blanco, the court administrator, told Lorenzo that that would happen in about an hour.

In the meantime, Lorenzo and Alberto stepped out into the hall to find Porten. He was standing next to a window looking out at the plaza, smoking a cigarette. They greeted one another, with embraces, pats on the back, and shouts of *"mi amigo."*

"I'm really glad to see you," whispered Lorenzo, amid purposely loud questions of "How is mama?" and "Did papa go to the doctor?" To onlookers, they were brothers or cousins catching up on family business. They sat down on a bench.

"You remember my son, Alberto?" Lorenzo asked Porten. The young assistant looked startled at first, then smiled and joined the ruse.

"Of course, but he has become a man since I saw him last!" Porten said.

"Good to see you again, *tio*. Papa speaks of you often," Alberto said with an amused glimmer in his eye.

"Okay, sergeant, as much as I am relieved to see you, I have to ask, what are you doing here?" said Lorenzo.

"I'm on a mission," he said in a low voice.

"A mission to . . . ." Lorenzo stopped

talking. "Don't tell me the illusive . . ."

"Don't say his name out loud! Yes, I do mean who I think you mean."

Alberto looked thoroughly confused.

"I'll explain later. What's the plan?"

Porten glanced nervously around before saying in a loud voice—in Spanish—I hope to see you at grandpa's birthday celebration next week. He'll be very disappointed if you don't show up."

"I know, I know. But I'm a very busy man these days—and so is my son." As if on cue, Alberto nodded vigorously and said "*Sí, sí, sí.*"

Porten leaned closer to Lorenzo. "Can you leave now without going back to the embassy, I mean do you have your passport and all the legal papers for this trial with you?"

Lorenzo patted his briefcase. "It's all in here."

"How about you, Alberto?"

"I travel light, always."

"Passport?"

"That too."

"Good. Meet me in the courtyard of the building in one hour. Maxine will be transported back to Guayaquil by an official van. It will be normal for you to accompany her to the door to make sure she is safely on her way. Do that, and then walk out into the main square and into the first street on the left. A small dark sports sedan will be parked there. Here are the keys. Get into it and drive slowly around the plaza like tourists. I'll be along as soon as I can."

"What about Bobbi? I can't leave without her."

Porten thought for a moment. "Of course, although I am hesitant to take along an older person who might be . . ."

"Hard to handle," laughed Lorenzo. "Bobbi's an actress. If I frame this whole thing as if it was a movie role, she'll be fine. I just hope she has her passport with her."

They parted with the same familial gestures.

"Let's go see how Maxine is doing," said Lorenzo.

As they walked down the hall, Alberto touched Lorenzo's arm and pointed to a figure approaching from the other direction.

"How does it feel to lose so badly," Margo hissed. "Your washed up girl friend's gonna' die in Litoral. You chose her over me. I could have opened so many doors that you would have wound up in high office. President maybe." Her eyes filled with tears.

"Why did you do all of this to someone you didn't even know?"

"I knew enough to spot a kidnapper!"

"It was interesting to meet you, Margo. I appreciate your hospitality and also that you made Bobbi very happy with all that you arranged for her."

"That ungrateful bitch! I should have known her time had passed long ago."

Margo turned and walked away, her high heels clicking on the polished tile floors of the court building.

WITH BOBBI'S HELP, Maxine looked even a bit better. Her hair was combed again and makeup applied to hide the dark circles under her eyes. She was sitting on a cot when Lorenzo walked into the cell.

"Feeling better? You look a lot better."

"Thanks to Bobbi," she said, grabbing the older woman's hand and squeezing it.

Bobbi patted her on the shoulder. "I once played a kindly guard in a movie set in a women's prison."

"It's good that you can apply your old roles to everyday life," said Lorenzo with a slight sarcastic edge to his voice. I guess tender Bobbi is still self-centered Bobbi at heart, he thought.

"That sounded crass," she said, as if reading the look on his face. "Helping you has been a pleasure. You've been through so much, more than could be written in any movie script."

Blanco, the court administrator, appeared at the door. "It is time to go, *señorita*. The van is waiting."

Maxine walked forward on wobbly legs, supported by both Bobbi and Lorenzo. Alberto followed with her duffle bag of ratty clothes. "May I leave my nice dress on?" asked Maxine in a weak voice.

Blanco hesitated, presumably because that would be against the rules.

"*¿Cómo no?*" he said with a slight shrug.

At the door, two guards waited to guide her into the van. Lorenzo could have sworn he had seen one of them before. He shook off the memory. Not possible.

The van drove off with Maxine looking forlornly out a small window in the back door. Lorenzo took hold of Bobbi's arm and pulled her with him to the plaza which was filled with people having lunch and enjoying the sunshine. Alberto followed.

"You got your passport with you?"

"Yes," she said, a quizzical look on her face. "But why . . ."

"Don't ask. Just follow me."

The three walked at a rapid pace across the plaza and into the side street Porten had mentioned. They got into the sleek sedan. "You drive, Berto, and I'll navigate. Bobbi, is it too cramped back there?"

"No, my darling, it is fine. There's enough room back here and even a nice blanket in case I get cold."

Alberto stifled a smile. "My darling?" he whispered.

"Just drive!"

"But where to?"

"Just drive slowly around the plaza."

On their second pass, Lorenzo spied Porten sitting at a table in an outdoor café, pretending to read a newspaper.

"Isn't that your friend?" said Bobbi, "The one I saw you talking to?"

"Pull up next to where he is sitting," said Lorenzo. He stepped out onto the street and got into the back next to Bobbi. Porten slid into the passenger seat.

"Lorenzo, Alberto, Miss Bouquet, I need to tell you that we're about to do something very dangerous. I mean that both politically and physically."

"You can call me Bobbi."

"Thank you, Bobbi. Okay, here is the plan. We will drive to the town of Manta, which is on the Pacific Coast usually about one hour away. But we'll need to go over some back country roads that I know so it will take longer. I've got to make sure we aren't being followed."

"I assume we'll be leaving the country from there?" asked Lorenzo.

"Let's not get ahead of ourselves," said Porten.

"Bad guys will be behind us?" asked Alberto.

"Possibly."

"Cool."

"It reminds me of a movie released in the fifties with Clark Gable and Gene Tierney called *Never Let Me Go*," said Bobbi. "He was an American reporter stationed in Moscow and she was a Russian ballerina. They get married but are not able to stay together because of the Iron Curtain. She escapes in a fast car which, at one point, goes onto a drawn bridge as it is being raised. The car goes into the water. Very romantic. Really thrilling. I knew Gene well, but Gable eluded me. That bastard!"

"Whatever! Back to the plan," said Lorenzo.

"Sorry for the diversion," said Bobbi sheepishly.

"That's about all I want to say at this point," said Porten. "I will tell you that Maxine March is part of this plan."

Lorenzo breathed a sigh of relief. He trusted Porten so didn't ask any more questions.

At first, they stayed on the main highway which, though full of potholes, was otherwise paved. They dozed or exchanged small talk for about an hour.

"Someone's behind us," said Alberto. "Guys in a pickup. Bad guys in a pickup. Like in the jungle before."

Porten turned around. "Shit! MS-13! They've got better intelligence than we thought. Turn in here and douse the lights."

Alberto swerved the car quickly onto what looked like a jungle path. It was not paved and full of ruts and tree roots and so narrow the brush scraped the sides.

"Goodbye paint job," said Alberto.

"Pull in here."

He turned the car into brush so thick it closed behind the vehicle once it had passed through.

Porten put a finger to his lips. "We may have lost them," he whispered.

They heard no sounds as they sat quietly for ten minutes. Porten gave a thumbs up and Alberto reached for the ignition.

A branch cracked. An animal? A bird?

Just then, gunfire filled the air. Birds in the trees flew away en masse and Bobbi fainted.

49

LORENZO, ALBERTO, AND PORTEN GOT OUT OF THE CAR with their hands up.

"Rapido! Rapido!" yelled one of the men, motioning for them to step away from the car. Fortunately, they could not see Bobbi, slumped in the back seat and out of sight because of the tinted window glass.

"I know all about you, *maricón!"* said a voice, in perfect English. "From my compatriots. They had plenty to say before you murdered them."

"Your English is good, *mi amigo . . .*

"I am not your *amigo, señor!"*

"Did you learn that English when you were a kid growing up in L.A.?

"Shut up!" he hissed. "You know nothing of that!"

"Yes, I do, *señor,"* said Lorenzo. "I grew up in East L.A. too."

He raised his gun. "I said, shut up!" He swung the gun toward him, but Lorenzo ducked out of the way in time to avoid being hit.

"LORENZO, WATCH OUT!" yelled Porten.

The thug took another swing at Lorenzo's head but missed again.

Lorenzo was undeterred and kept talking. "What do you want of us? We are merely traveling to Manta."

"I think we both know that is a lie. But I don't care where you are going. You

won't be getting there anytime soon. When we get through with you, you will wish that you had never been born."

"Your quarrel is with me," said Lorenzo. "Let my friends go. I will face you alone. It's only right. They had nothing to do with why you are after me. Okay?"

"Not okay." He nodded at his four compatriots, two of whom stepped behind Alberto and Porten, their knives poised against their throats.

At that point, shots rang out and all five men, including the leader, were shot in the backs of their heads.

"What kept you?" said Porten.

Five men wearing camouflage uniforms walked over to him and gave him high-five greetings. "We thought you needed a little scare," said one of the men.

"I'll scare YOU!" said Porten, a scowl on his face. Then his face broke into a big smile and all five men embraced.

"We should get moving," said Porten. "I don't want to get behind schedule."

"Will someone please tell me what is going on?" said a weak voice from the car.

Bobbi Bouquet was stirring. She crawled out of the back seat and smoothed her dress.

"Now who are all these handsome men?" she said, eyelids fluttering.

"Men," said Porten, "meet Miss Bobbi Bouquet, a famous movie star."

The men looked puzzled at first, until one of them walked over to Bobbi and kissed her hand. The others did so too. Bobbi nearly swooned. "How grand! All these young guys and me the only gal! What more can I ask for?"

Even though the men probably had never heard of Bobbi, they reacted to the word 'star' and thrust pieces of paper in her direction.

"Make it out to my mom. Her name is Sandy."

"Make it out to Kimberly."

"Make it out to Angie."

"Make it out to Mable."

"Dear, that doesn't sound like a modern name."

"It's for my grandma. I figured she'd know who you are."

"Yes, dear, of course. I understand."

"Okay, okay," said Porten. "We've got to get a move on. Let's load 'em up."

"What about the bodies, sarge?"

Fortunately, Bobbi was standing away from the pile of corpses. Lorenzo pulled her back toward the car. She didn't need to see all of that carnage.

"Dig some shallow graves and throw them in there," yelled Porten. "The animals will dig them up and take care of things for us."

As Lorenzo helped Bobbi into the car, she whispered, "I guess you didn't think I saw all those bodies, my darling. When you're my age, death is nothing to fear. Besides, there were many more bodies than that in that zombie movie I did ten years ago."

"WE'RE OUTTA' HERE!" shouted Porten, and they soon were.

50

AS PORTEN'S MEN DISAPPEARED INTO THE JUNGLE, Lorenzo and the others got back to the car and were soon back on the main highway. After a few miles, Porten answered a radio call.

"Okay, great. See you in a few." He turned around. "I've got a big surprise for you," he said, a big grin on his face. "There, pull into that trail." Alberto slowed down and then followed Porten's directions.

"About a half mile and . . .. Presto! Look what we have here."

Sitting in the middle of the narrow trail was the supposedly official prison van that Maxine had gotten into for her return to the prison.

"Porten, you are a miracle worker!" said a smiling Lorenzo. "How did you . . ."

"If I told you, etc. etc.," laughed Porten.

Lorenzo, Bobbi, and Alberto got out of the car and ran to the van. Porten's men stood by the side of the vehicle, dressed in uniforms with the words *Prisiónes de Ecuador* on the front.

"You guys are great," said Lorenzo, shaking hands with each of the men. "Thank you."

The back door to the van was open and Lorenzo could see Maxine lying on a cot inside. "Bobbi, do your stuff as a nurse," he said.

Bobbi climbed into the van and sat down beside Maxine. She held Maxine's

head up so she could drink water. She felt her forehead. "She's burning up with fever. Bring me a wet towel." She glanced at Lorenzo. "She needs to see a doctor!"

He nodded and turned to Porten. "Sergeant, how far are we from Manta?"

"About ten kilometers."

"Can we get Maxine to a hospital when we get there?"

"Not advisable," he said. "By now, the Ecuadorians know that your friend is not on her way to Litoral. They'll be looking for her."

"So what do we do?"

"I have a place in mind where we'll all be safe, at least for a while."

"Sounds good to me," he said. "Let's go!"

Bobbi had stepped out of the van. "I want to stay with Maxine. She needs me."

Lorenzo looked at Porten, who was the leader in charge of this escapade. "Good idea. Keep her quiet until we get to where we're going."

Lorenzo, Alberto, and Porten got back into the car. At the sergeant's signal, Alberto let the van drive ahead of them.

"Keep them in sight but hang back a bit," Porten said. "This flashy car could attract attention, and we don't want the police to stop them if it stops us. Make sense?" Both Alberto and Lorenzo nodded.

"Are you ever planning to fill me in about where we're going?"

"In due time, Lorenzo. In due time."

51

THEY DROVE FOR ANOTHER HALF HOUR carrying on in idle chit chat—their backgrounds, their families, etc. Although Lorenzo had a lot of important questions to ask Porten, he respected the man's mission timetable. He would fill him in due time.

"Okay, enough of this secrecy stuff," said Porten as they drove into Manta. "Manta has the largest seaport in Ecuador. It has existed since pre-Columbian times. It was a trading post and, because of the harbor, the perfect spot for explorers to land and go inland to Quito, plundering along the way."

"That sounds familiar," scoffed Alberto. "There's always plenty of plundering where my people are concerned."

"Mine too," said Lorenzo.

"I should speak up for white people but I can't see why," laughed Porten. "Anyway, to continue my background report. Fishing, especially for tuna, is the main economic activity. Plus tourism. Cruise ships stop here regularly. Manta also has an international airport and, adjacent to that is Manta Air Base. That's where we're headed."

"This is beginning to make a lot of sense," said Lorenzo. "Go on."

"Between 1999 and 2009, the air base was used by the U.S. Air Force to support anti-narcotics military operations throughout Latin America. A lot of surveillance flights over Colombia

that spied on the drug cartels started here. Then the government of Ecuador changed and a new president, a guy named Rafael Correa, was elected in 2006. One of his main campaign promises was to kick the U.S. out. When the lease on the base was up, he did just that and the U.S. left. Almost."

"Why do I think the 'almost' involves the CIA and DEA," said Lorenzo.

Porten smiled. "Slow down and pull over here."

Ahead Lorenzo could see the main gate of the base. The van had driven up to the gate but had been stopped by a uniformed soldier. First only one soldier was talking to the driver, then others quickly surrounded the vehicle.

"Lorenzo, stay here. Alberto, pretend to be my translator." The two of them got out of the car and walked towards the van.

"HALT!" yelled the man who had stopped the van. Three others ran back to Porten and Alberto and patted them down. A fourth soldier saw Lorenzo in the car and motioned for him to get out. He was also patted down and herded with a rifle over to the other two.

The first man, apparently an officer, walked over to the three. He did not speak English. Then began the laborious process of the officer and Porten talking to one another with Alberto translating.

Porten told them that he had been sent by his government to return a wanted prisoner to the U.S. She had gotten sick so was in the ambulance ahead. They were going to wait for a plane to take them out of Ecuador.

"Why is she in a prison van and not a real ambulance?" asked the officer.

"Both governments want to get her out of your country very quietly." Hopefully, Ecuador did not have anything like an APB with Maxine's name on it.

"Who are these other people?"

"My translator, Alberto . . ." Alberto raised his hand, as if in school . . .

"And the poor woman's husband, Sancho. He's a bit crazy in the head."

Lorenzo angled his head to one side and let his jaw drop and looked as though he might drool. He then let out a grunt and a moan, Quasimodo style. The officer was unconvinced and, at his signal, his men cocked their rifles and started to herd Lorenzo and the others to another van parked nearby.

"What about the prisoner?" said Porten. "You can't leave her here. Do you want to take the responsibility of what happens to her?"

The officer held up his hand and walked over to the van. He opened the rear door and looked in carefully as if expected something bad to lash out. Bobbi was sitting by Maxine's cot mopping her brow. She had fashioned one of her silk scarfs so that it looked like a nurse's cap.

"What is the meaning of this?" she said in such a commanding tone that the officer stepped back. Alberto ran up to translate.

"I am dealing with a very sick woman," she continued. "Do you want her death on your hands?"

"*Dios mío!*" The officer crossed himself and walked back to the others, still surrounded by soldiers with cocked rifles.

"STAND DOWN, RODRIGUEZ!" said a voice. "CUT THE NO SPEAKY INGLES CRAP!" They all turned to see a tall man in jungle fatigues walking towards them. Four others dressed the same way were behind him. All were carrying rifles.

When the officer saw the man, he smiled and walked over to him. They embraced and everybody relaxed. Guns were lowered and cigarettes came out. The big man and Rodriguez talked amiably for a while, with lots of laughing and punching each other in the shoulder.

After five minutes or so of that, the big man turned to face Porten, Lorenzo, and Alberto. "You can relax," he said. "Just follow me." The big man turned and climbed into the pickup his men had just driven up in.

Alberto closed the rear door of the van and walked back to the car with Porten and Lorenzo following. They got in.

"Who the hell was that?" said Lorenzo.

"You'll soon find out," said Porten, a smile on his face.

52

THE SMALL CONVOY FOLLOWED THE PICKUP through the main gate and across the tarmac of the airfield to a group of Quonset huts that looked like they'd been there since World War II. The big man got out and walked to the rear of the van. He opened the door, greeted Bobbi, and helped her out.

She walked over to Lorenzo who hugged her. "You were magnificent," he whispered.

"You might call it the role of a lifetime," she said, a sad look on her face. "I had to do something. Your friend is dying."

"I know," he said, tears in his eyes.

They watched as the big man knelt down next to Maxine and gently slid an arm under her head.

"Maxie, my wonderful Maxie. Why did I let our lives go so bad? I should have been there for you and the boy. I told myself that I did it for my career. The real reason was that I couldn't commit to you or anyone. We were good together. I've let you down. Causing all these problems by taking the boy and then leaving you to clean up my mess."

"I've taken good care of our boy," she said in a weak voice. "You should see Tito now. He's real smart and doing well. That's all thanks to Lorenzo."

She gazed out the door but did not seem to be able to focus or even see clearly. "Lorenzo? Is Lorenzo nearby?"

"I'm here, Maxine. Your boy is

waiting for you at home in Oregon."

Maxine started coughing. The big man handed her a hand-kerchief and she held it to her mouth. When she took it away it was covered in blood.

"Lorenzo, this is Paul Bickford. He rescued Tito from his hellish life here and brought him to me. He's his father, like I'm his mother. You're his other father. A boy is lucky to have two fathers, don't you think?"

Bickford put out his hand and they shook.

"Lorenzo Madrid."

They looked down at Maxine who was having trouble breathing. "I've sent for a doctor," said Bickford.

He stepped out of the van and motioned Porten over. "You've done good, sergeant. Real good."

"Thank you, sir. I have to say how glad I am to see you. Your plan was working up to a point, but I was beginning to have my doubts."

He turned to Lorenzo and Alberto.

"Paul, this is Alberto Dragón," said Lorenzo. "He's been my right hand man since I've been here."

"And who is this magnificent lady," said Bickford, turning toward a forlorn looking Bobbi, not used to being out of the spotlight. Her face brightened and she pulled off her nurse's kerchief. "Bobbi Bouquet, colonel. I have wanted to meet you formally since I first saw you."

Bickford walked over to her and kissed her hand. "How grand," she said, linking her arm in his as they walked back to where the others were standing.

"Were you ever a nurse?" asked Bickford.

"Oh no, but I played one once or twice in the past in such films as *Battle Fatigue* and *Nurse Under Fire*.

"Oh, you're **that** Bobbi Bouquet!" said Bickford. "My mom loved your movies."

"I'll bet she did," said Bobbi, disengaging her arm from his.

"Okay," said Bickford. "Here's the plan. In about one hour, a helicopter will land and take the three of you—Lorenzo, Bobbi, and . . . what's your name again . . ."

"Alberto Dragón."

"Sure, sorry, my mind's a blank sometimes. The bird'll fly you out of here to a U.S. Navy cruiser that just happens to be sailing up the coast. The ship'll take you to the Panama Canal and a base we have there. Then to L.A. and you're on your own from there."

He turned to Alberto. "You got a passport?"

"Yes sir, I have dual citizenship. I'll be going to Miami where I've got family."

"Good, I'll see if I can get you there from L.A."

He turned to Lorenzo. "You want to see Maxine again before you leave?"

"Yeah, I do."

He walked over to the van and climbed in, kneeling down next to Maxine. She was breathing hard and her eyes were closed. "Maxine, it's Lorenzo. Paul's called for a doctor and he'll be here soon and when you get well, you can . . ."

"Don't humor me, Lorenzo. We both know that I'm dying. Words can't express my gratitude to you for taking care of Tito. He's lucky to have you by his side. He'll grow up to be a fine man . . ." She started coughing again and closed her eyes.

Lorenzo dabbed his eyes as he walked over to Bobbi and Alberto. The three embraced and looked up as the whirring sounds of rotors signaled the approach of the helicopter. They grabbed their small bags and walked quickly to the aircraft, keeping their heads down to avoid the blades.

Bickford turned to Lorenzo. "Thank you, Lorenzo. You are a great man. Someday, when Tito is old enough to understand, will you tell him about me? That I tried to be a brave soldier and help my country, but along the way I let down the ones I loved."

Lorenzo shook Bickford's hand again, but the big man pulled him into a tight embrace.

"I'll only tell him the first part—about you being a brave soldier who lived to help his country. And I'll ad lib a bit and tell him that you're the man who saved him."

"No, Lorenzo, you saved him."

They parted, Lorenzo walked to the helicopter, and was helped aboard by a crew member. "Here you go, sir."

As the craft took off, Lorenzo waved at the disappearing figure of Paul Bickford. He thought he saw a salute but was not sure.

❏ ❏ ❏ ❏ ❏

Several weeks later, a package arrived at Lorenzo's office from the American embassy in Quito. In it were: an Ecuadorian birth certificate, a silk purse, some beaded jewelry, several small silver-framed photos, and a Panama hat just Tito's size.

The End